In Pursuit of the Elusive
Dream — Utopia

In Pursuit of the Elusive Dream — Utopia

Ernest S.

To Dale,
I truly appreciate
your friendship,

Ernie

iUniverse, Inc.
New York Lincoln Shanghai

In Pursuit of the Elusive Dream — Utopia

iUniverse, Inc.

For information address:
iUniverse, Inc.
2021 Pine Lake Road, Suite 100
Lincoln, NE 68512
www.iuniverse.com

ISBN: 0-595-29518-5 (pbk)
ISBN: 0-595-75022-2 (cloth)

Printed in the United States of America

Contents

Acknowledgement

I had thought to write about my life's odyssey for years; however, I could not have done it without the encouragement of some very close friends.

My long time friend Gary a Vietnam war veteran, and a Republican through and through, who now lives in Canada. He has helped me tremendously in regards to contact potential publishers, has tried very hard to teach a reluctant me, how to use his computer. Although our philosophies on world politics differ greatly, he has been most supportive in getting this book published. Gary realizes that I am not and never will be anti-American, just anti-President Bush's policies. So we have agreed not to discuss politics, and respect each others view points.

My friends Carol and Lee in B.C. who have made me a part of their close family circle, their weekly calls have become a source of strength when I felt down and sometimes sorry for myself. Their eighty-seven year old mom, who is a bundle of energy and who has been an inspiration to me, for she too has had a hard life but never complains.

Mikki and Anne who were my biggest support when I had cancer, and gave me a home when I was homeless during that time. They kept my mind off my difficulties by including me in many activities, from ski-dooing to ice-fishing and playing cards.

The Pipke family, (Leanne, Terry, Clark, Carl, and Lane and their parents Jack (who recently passed away) and Ella (who encountered some of the same wartime experiences that I had to endure before she immigrated to Canada), I am proud to call them friends. Not only are they a perfect family but also the perfect neighbour to have.

And, last but not least, my Norwegian Elkhound, Cujo, who was a present from Mikki and Anne as a little puppy. He has now become my companion and buddy. He makes me laugh with his little antics. Have you ever seen the sight of an old man, rolling around and wrestling with his dog in the deep snow? Well that is Cujo. He keeps me young and active.

Despite all the hardships and sorrows, this is still a wonderful world because of friends like you.

Preface

✦

Musings of a Seventy Year Old Man

This book contains the musings of a seventy year old man who has never written a book before and therefore does not know what the end result will be, nor if it will ever be finished.

Why then, you may ask, is this old fool even attempting to write a book? I have questioned the purpose and the reasoning for many years myself; that's right, many years, for I have been thinking about it for at least twenty-five to thirty years. However, I have always found excuses galore not to write it at all. Some of the excuses are as follows:

1. Vocabulary—you see English is not my first language.

2. The subject matter—my life has been so eventful and my experiences so many that there is a danger of producing a book that is a collection of thoughts, happenings and innuendos that may confuse the reader and lose his/her interest. For although with age I have slowed down, my mind is racing at all times; going back and forth over the more than sixty years of good and bad experiences.

3. Over the years I have become quite cynical, opinionated, and disillusioned about life in general, and the reason why the human race inhabits this earth. Thus, the danger exists that this book may focus too much on my own opinions and feelings, but I believe that the reader will recognize that I have earned the right to express these feelings, opinions and, to some extent, philosophies on life and the human race in general.

This book will touch on many issues, such as: Love, Hate, Tolerance, Racism, Justice, Fairness, Death, War, Sex, Religion, the Death Penalty, Mercy Killings, and above all, Integrity, Honesty, and Dreams. Dreams of hope for the future of the universe and for us the human race. For no matter who or what we are, young or old, rich or poor, what race, creed or status, we must all be allowed to be able to dream. Without dreams we may as well be dead.

So, finally, I have been able to remove most barriers in my mind and decided this book must be written, regardless if anyone will ever read it or form an opinion on it. It must be written for numerous reasons.

1. Every human being on this earth has a story to tell, everyone is a somebody, the majority of us may be unknown to the general public, but many of us have lived a life full of experiences; tragic, humorous, full of love, loveless, isolated or among friends, with or without families, heroic and sometimes dull. Whatever our lives may be, I know that compared to autobiographies in books or films about the stars, heroes, politicians, authors, film-makers and many others, my life has been much more eventful and taught me so much that I have to put it on paper.

2. Stories about the Second World War have been very one-sided. The sufferings of the people on the losing side, in this case the Germans, have been completely ignored. I am talking about the German civilians, the slaughter and rape of children, women and old people. I must talk about some of those happenings sixty years ago, as I was born in Eastern Europe of German parents. I promise not to use any rhetoric or propaganda. I shall talk about my own personal experiences only.

3. The last reason I am compelled to write this book is that I am the last member of a family whose history and family tree goes back nearly 800 years to the days when the Christian Crusaders invaded Eastern Europe to spread the gospel in parts of the Baltic countries, Russia, and Poland. Many stayed, including my ancestors, and I intend to leave something behind that proves that I existed.

I strongly believe that the main reason for us being here is to contribute in some way, no matter how small, to make this a better world to live in. I hope that I have tried my best to have contributed, as I have always fought for the underdog and the underprivileged. I have always worked on behalf of children at risk and for their families.

However, a book about the cruelties of war, any war, a book on the wrong of dishonesty, propaganda, abuse of power and wealth, may contribute a little more to save this world, even if only a few people read it and carry the torch, I would have accomplished something. Taking away the freedom of people to choose their own destinies, killing, starving people in the name of democracy or religion, invading other countries because they want to be different or because we need or want their natural resources; is wrong. It can only lead to the destruction of our universe.

Friends have accused me of living in Utopia and that may be so, however, I wouldn't be surprised to find that the majority of the world's population would love to live in Utopia. It most certainly would be preferable to living in a world that is dominated by hunger for power, wealth and superiority. Greed breeds more greed. Power breeds a hunger for more power. Invasions and suppressions breed more of the same.

I very much believe in and live by Max Ehrmann's "Desiderata","You are a child of the universe, and you have a right to be here." I would like to add that you have a right to live where you want to live, how you want to live, with whom you want to live.

The biggest obstacle to live in Utopia is that the majority of the world population are followers; easily led by propaganda, promises and manipulations. We are too lazy to put our mind to work, form our own opinions, enter into discussions no matter how controversial, and above all, use common sense. But no—We find it much easier to conform to one doctrine, dogma, or philosophy. It is so much easier to be one of the masses. Just as many people use religion, any denomination, as a crutch to be able to face adversity and hardship, we feel more secure in being part of the majority, and follow a dominant, persuasive leader. It matters not if we are led toward destruction and into oblivion.

PART I

1

Today's Issues and My Views

To live in Utopia is to live in a world of perfection, and I am realistic enough to know that this will never happen. But is it too much to ask humanity to strive for perfection, and to work toward a common goal of peace and togetherness; of sharing and caring? To work toward the elimination of poverty, persecution, and sickness; but above all, to work toward the elimination of war, aggression, and dominance of the weak. "How?" you ask.

1. Elimination of nuclear weapons.

Every country and every government must agree to abolish and never rebuild nuclear weapons or any other weapons of mass destruction. This includes the U.S.A. and Israel. This process will take decades, and must be closely supervised by an international body. Attempts had been made during the Kennedy era, but failed after some initial success. The failure was due to greed, due to the power of a few involved in the oil production, due to the corruption and short-sightedness of those we look up to. But, it is mainly due to the demise of the Soviet Union, and the emergence of the U.S.A. as the only super power in this world, who thumbs its nose at the rest of the world, and does what it pleases, when it pleases, "To hell with world opinion".

God bless America. He blesses America because it is the land of the free and the home of the brave. As a child, I have heard enough propaganda and rhetoric from Hitler and Dr. Goebbels, his propaganda minister, to last me a life-time. What I hear today from President Bush and Mr. Rumsfeld, however, takes the cake. What they use as propaganda is hard to swallow, and should be unbeliev-able to anyone with a little common sense. It is sickening when at major sports events, such as football and baseball, beer-guzzling, pot-bellied fans, wrapped in American flags, yell "God bless America."

Is it any wonder that God has no time to listen to starving and dying children, particularly in third world countries; or countries that are embargoed, because the American president does not agree with these countries doctrines or policies? God looks the other way when innocent Israelis and Palestinians are killed each day; or when Protestants ambush Catholics, or visa versa, in Ireland. Did you ever notice that as far back as we can remember God fought in all wars? During the Second World War the German soldiers' belt buckles were inscribed, "Gott mit uns," God is with us. The American's inscription said, "In God we trust."

In the 12th and 13th century, the Christian Crusaders brought Christianity to the unbelievers in Africa and Eastern Europe, and in the process, slaughtered children, women, and elders by the thousands. This was repeated in the 16th and 17th centuries with North and South American natives, although their spirituality was superior to that of the so called Christians.

I beg the reader's forgiveness, for I have digressed a little from how to strive toward a peaceful existence, although our beliefs and that of other peoples come to play in this plan. I suggested that the abolishment of all nuclear weapons was item number one.

The trillions of dollars saved from total disarmament would be spent on the elimination of poverty, on rebuilding and the stabilization of third world countries, for it is us, and our fore-fathers who are to blame for their present situation. Future wars will only worsen the present status. I would like to remind the reader that this was written prior to an American invasion of Iraq, which will happen within the next year, against world opinion, whether or not the weapons inspectors in Iraq will find weapons of mass destruction. To those hell-bent for war, I would like to say this. Anyone who has lived through the horrors of the second world war, who has experienced and seen the slaughter, rape and persecution of millions of innocent people, who has watched the destruction of one thousand year old cities, cities that were known for their beauty, culture, and irreplaceable buildings and art; cities that had no military targets within their walls. Anyone who has lived through this madness would say, "Never again!"

We in North America feel so smug, we are so far away from all these happenings that we applaud Mr. Bush's push for further wars, and believe me, Iraq is not the end of it. "We are the power and we are so superior, what does it matter if children and other civilians get killed? That is part of war. Our boys are safe in their high-tech planes." Isn't it exciting to watch on television? It's just like watching fireworks.

2. Reorganization by continents.

Continents must unite, just as Europe endeavours to do now. Although good, old England does not yet want to completely become a European state within a European parliament, they have not yet accepted the fact that the days of colonialism are over. That is why Mr. Blair feels secure in being Mr. Bush's lap-dog in the hope that the U.S.A. will prevent England from swallowing the bitter pill to become part of a united Europe.

There should be six, not five, united continents, each with one common currency and their own parliament. Although individual countries will have their own government, they must work hand in hand with their continent's parliament in order to support fair trade with each other and in order to stabilize the economy, support weaker and poorer countries within their group. This is just as Europe is trying to do now. The continents that presently exist must agree to unite among themselves, and add a sixth group, that of a united Central and South America.

A world structure such as this would eliminate the selling out by politicians to big corporations, thereby excluding corruption. Politicians would be elected based on their capabilities, not their bank accounts. It will eliminate terrorism and wars. It will increase prosperity, learning, and social standing. We produce enough food and medication to support the world population. Today's third world countries possess enough natural resources to benefit their population. It must be explored and produced, and not just to enrich some sheiks, dictators, and princelings.

All this would lead to a better world. If we continue on our present path, however, the world as we know it will self-destruct. History has shown that empires and super powers eventually fall; because they cannot harness their hunger for more power.

3. Other issues.

Not as pressing as the first two are of importance, and I do have an opinion on those. I have said at the outset of my musings that I am opinionated, but these opinions are based on life experience, common sense, and a lot of thinking. If nothing else, these writings are meant to encourage my fellow human beings to think for themselves, to form their own opinions and to make themselves heard, not blindly follow a leader who may lead us into oblivion.

What do I get out of this? The satisfaction that an average Joe can make himself heard and hopefully contributes something that may benefit future generations. I am growing old. I have survived many horrors during my childhood, as you will see in the next chapter. I have survived cancer and other illnesses. But I have never lost my belief in mankind.

4. Global warming.

The ecology—the preservation of our forests and other natural resources. The Kyoto Accord: cleaning up our rivers and lakes, restrictions on fishing and hunting, reforestation, etc. are small and often isolated attempts by some governments, to stem the tide of mass pollution, the erosion of the ozone layer, and the rapid meltdown of the Arctic ice.

These feeble attempts are not going to cut it. Unless every government is committed to implement, among other things, the Kyoto Accord, we are headed for disaster. Again it's the U.S.A. that objects and even a small province in Canada, like Alberta which is a major oil producer is against implementation of the accord. Why? It's because the oil companies are against it, and use scare tactics to convince the public that Kyoto is bad. Everyone lives for today, profits today and to hell with future generations. Unless we start conservation in our own homes, drive smaller cars, use public transportation more often, recycle waste and other materials on a regular basis, we will not succeed. Every single person must do it. Every town and city must do it. Every country must do it. It is a universal issue; therefore it will only work if everybody is committed to it.

As usual, the most industrialized countries are the main polluters, and they are the ones that object the most. Surveys and polls have shown that the majority of our population is in favour of Kyoto. However, when it comes to profits now, democracy flies out the window.

5. Euthanasia (mercy killing).

Personally, I believe in it. Any human being that is terminally ill with no chance of recovery should be able to ask a physician to terminate his/her life. If this person is a child or exists like a vegetable only, they should have the right to die, if their care-givers ask a physician to end their life of suffering. The decisions should be left to a panel of physicians, they should not hide behind a Hippocratic Oath that they must preserve life under any circumstance.

If it is me that is terminally ill, and I wanted to die, I would say it is my life, it is my body, and no government can forbid me to end my suffering. Just as women say, it is my body, if I want an abortion, I will have one. And believe me, most people have a strong will to live, and will ask for euthanasia only as a last resort. By the way, I support abortions if the wellbeing of the mother or the physical or mental health of the unborn is at risk. Abortions as a means of birth control should be illegal. Every person of childbearing or child producing age has all kinds of artificial birth control available.

6. The death penalty.

The death penalty is a deterrent to commit capital crimes. Although personally I would rather die than spend a lifetime in prison, the majority of prisoners would prefer to receive a life sentence, as there is always a glimmer of hope to be set free, or to escape, as it may be. Having said that, I believe the death penalty should be carried out only in cases of premeditated murder that can be proven beyond any reasonable doubt, whatsoever. For the rape and murder of children under the age of fourteen, and for the killing of police officers, while performing their duties to protect the public. Once convicted, the criminal should be allowed one appeal only, and the death penalty sentence should be carried out within one year of the conviction.

7. Racism and Tolerance.

Everyone is a bigot; it matters not whether you are Caucasian, African-American, Native American, Oriental, Palestinian, or any other race. The word 'tolerance' itself is wrong. It means we will tolerate somebody, even if we dislike that person. Of course, I will never admit to being a bigot, and neither will the majority of people. As long as we notice the difference in peoples' colour, facial structures, hair styles, or even the difference in clothing and dress, we somehow discriminate against that other human being. The only people who are incapable of bigotry are small children.

For example, we see Yasser Arafat as an ugly man with a funny headdress, therefore he cannot be trusted. Sikhs with their turbans are the same. African Americans are in most cases lazy, live off the avails of pimping or other criminal activities. The only thing they are good at is music and sports. Native Americans are not too bright, they are all alcoholics, and cannot be trusted. Orientals are sly, they are all gamblers, and they will cheat the white man, and most are involved in gang activities.

All this, of course, is hidden in our minds, and we will not dare to openly admit it. Although I imagine and assume people of different races feel exactly the same about us Caucasians. The best examples of proof that this is, and always will be a major problem are jurors in criminal court that have to find an accused of different origin than their own, guilty or not guilty.

How can we overcome these feelings? for that is what they are. I honestly don't know, for it is human nature to notice the difference in people first, rather than see the beauty, goodness and kindness that is inside all of us. All we can do is to fight these inner feelings, through integrity, openness and honesty within ourselves.

8. Religion.

Native Americans don't call it beliefs or religion; they call it spirituality, and I am much more comfortable with that. Also their doctrine of loving, sharing and caring, is much closer to my philosophy of what life is all about, and how we conduct ourselves.

Although all major world denominations preach love, I cannot really comment on Hinduism, Buddhism, or the Islamic religion, as I was never exposed to any of them. The native spirituality I have come to know and love, as I have worked with the native community for the past twenty years.

As a child, I grew up and believed the Roman Catholic dogma. When I learned about the evolution of man and started to think for myself, doubts entered my mind; particularly about the creation of Adam and Eve, and the immaculate conception of Mary. More doubts emerge when I studied history, which always was my favourite subject, and learned about the power of the church during the Holy Roman Empire in medieval times.

I do believe that Jesus Christ lived, and preached love, understanding and tolerance. He was in my mind a man to be admired. But look what happened with Christianity in centuries after his life. Popes, cardinals and the upper echelon of the church became excessively power hungry and greedy. They ordered the killings in the name of Christ. They practically abused every one of the Ten Commandments, and tried to cover it up by pomp, and beautiful emotionally charged church ceremonies. However, the biggest blow to my belief in the Catholic Church came when I saw the horrors of war, the killings of innocent children when I first came to know about the holocaust and the killings of more than six million Jews, gypsies, and homosexuals. How can a loving God let this happen?

Furthermore, the church, and therefore the pope, must take some blame for the death and starvation of millions of children as well as the physical and sexual abuse of children. Mainly because the pope will not modernize old doctrines; e.g. sex is to be indulged in for pro-creation only, birth control is against the teachings of the church, and priests are supposed to be celibate, and are not allowed to marry.

None of the above were teachings of Jesus Christ. I used to have feelings of guilt about my doubts. Not any more. I have come to believe that many people need the church as a crutch to face the hardship, adversity and illnesses in their lives. I don't. Life experience has made me a stronger human being. Caring for my fellowman, and the sharing and love I have to offer gives me a secure feeling, that if there is a life hereafter, which nobody knows, I will be accepted at the gates of Heaven.

2

My Childhood

I was born in Koenigsberg, which was the capital of East Prussia. Today it is called Kaliningrad and a part of Russia. East Prussia was a German province, but isolated from the mainland by the Polish Corridor, which was established after the First World War to give Poland access to the Baltic Sea. This province was bordered by Russia to the east, Poland to the south and west, the Baltic Sea to the north, and Lithuania to the north-east.

Koenigsberg, a city of approximately 500,000 in the late 1930's, became famous (or infamous) when toward the end of the second world war, January/February of 1945, German troops were determined to keep the Russian armies away from central Germany and Berlin as long as possible, to give the Allied armies of Eisenhower and Montgomery enough time to occupy Berlin first. Little did they know that Stalin, Churchill and Roosevelt had decided already at the Yalta Conference, how Germany should be divided, but more of that later.

The fighting lasted six weeks and Koenigsberg was completely demolished. The German soldiers who survived the battle were shipped to Siberia, most of them were never heard from again. I remember Koenigsberg as a beautiful, vibrant city. My mother took me there when I was eight years old. We visited King Frederick III of Prussia's palace, in particular to see the Bernstein Room (Amber Room). The walls of this huge room were made of solid amber which was gold-framed. It had been a gift of Czar Peter to King Frederick.

We lived in Tilsit, which is now Sovetsk, a quaint city of about eighty thousand people on the Memel (Njemen) River, which was the border with Lithuania. Tilsit made its mark in history when in 1807 Napoleon and King Frederick signed a peace treaty which officially ended the war between France and Prussia. Napoleon needed this treaty so that he could freely move into Russia, and toward Moscow, where he and his troops barely escaped the cold winter. This should have been a warning to Hitler one hundred and thirty years later.

Legend has it that Queen Louise, King Frederick's wife, had to sleep with Napoleon in order to get the treaty signed. The house where Queen Louise slept was still there. Legend has it that she inscribed a frost-covered window in her bedroom with a poem, as she could not sleep. She had used her diamond ring to do so. It follows: "Wer nie sein Brot mit Tranen asz, wer nie weinend auf dem bette sasz die langen einsamen Nachte, der kennt euch nicht ihr himmlischen Machte," loosely translated it means: "He who never ate his bread with tears in his eyes, he who never sat crying on his bed the long lonesome nights, does not know the powers of heaven."—Tilsit's other claim to fame is known world-wide and that, of course, is Tilsiter cheese.

My parents owned a large corner complex at Hohe Strasse and Ragnit Strasse, which over-looked the Memel River and the Queen Louise Bridge, which was a draw-bridge, and the Crusader Church (Lutheran), which was built around the fifteen hundreds. The church featured a beautiful three onion-shaped, tiered tower made of copper, which of course gleamed green in the sunlight. You could climb winding stairs inside the tower, and have a gorgeous view of the city. On a clear day you could almost see the Memel Delta near the Baltic Sea.

My parents owned a restaurant and a busy pub in the complex. Our plush living quarters were on the second floor. There were also four other businesses rented out by my father. On the Ragnit Strasse wing, there were a dozen apartments. The courtyard was huge and was equipped for farmers to park their wagons when they came to market or on other business. There were stables for their horses and my father employed stable-boys to look after them. He also employed two bartenders, several waiters, a chef, and a maid for our living quarters and to look after me. My parents had no time for their son.

That is my earliest recollection on how lonely I always was, craving for attention and for love. This loneliness and constant search for love would be with me for the rest of my life. It influenced and consumed my whole being during the next sixty odd years. It would dictate how I behaved and how I related to others. All my friendships, companionships, and even sexual relationships were driven and sustained by the desire to be loved, to be wanted, accepted and needed.

I have never found it, except for some brief, fleeting moments during my life. I am an old, lonely man who could never communicate his needs to others; except now that I have put it down on paper. Don't get me wrong, I am not bitter. In my own way, I am content, and most of the time I love my isolated life although there are days when I am depressed and have this unfulfilled feeling inside of me that I find very difficult to explain.

My father was a very stern man who believed in corporal punishment, by that I mean beatings. For the tiniest infraction, in most cases, imagined causes, or lies told him by my mother. He usually waited until nightfall, when I was in bed. He came to my room, lifted the covers and my nightgown and beat me over and over with our dog's leash, using the buckle end. My butt and upper legs were red and blue with welts and I was quite often bleeding. I never cried out, but shed many tears when I was alone.

A few years later when I reached puberty, I always felt embarrassed to lift my nightgown for these beatings. I almost felt vindicated when he had a stroke in 1942 and I was the one that assisted him to the bathroom to help him pee.

My mother was a beautiful woman; the Vivian Leigh-type. She was small, fine boned and the life of any party. Unfortunately, the beauty was only skin deep. She was quite snobbish, her days filled with beauty parlours, seamstresses, and planning for dinners, theatre and travel. She was very sharp-tongued with the help and most of the time ignored me. At that time, I still loved her, but now I believe it was more pride and admiration to have a mother who appeared in fashion magazines, and was the toast of the town. I will always remember her and my father preparing for the opera. My father in his tuxedo and my mother in an evening gown with a tiara in her hair, beauty personified. I tried to touch her or just stroke her hand softly, only to be pushed away. She snarled, "Stay away from me, your hands are dirty," although my hands were very clean. Oh, how I ached to be hugged and held by this beautiful woman, who was my mother.

I was not allowed to play with children in the neighbourhood, if they were not of the same social circle as my parents. I could never invite school chums to come home with me unless approved by my mother. My grandparents on my father's side were farmers, but lived quite far away. I only saw them twice in my life. Today I believe that my mother did not encourage visits with my father's family because they were below her standards.

My mother's parents owned a beautiful estate about thirty kilometres from Tilsit, which consisted of more than two hundred hectares of the best soil in all of Europe. A twenty-four room mansion with a terrace that led from the ballroom into a park with oak and elm trees that were centuries old. This estate had been in my ancestor's possession since Christian Crusaders invaded these parts of Europe in the twelfth and thirteenth centuries.

I spent most of my vacations there, surrounded by loving people, and free to do what I wanted. My grandparents, whom I called Oma and Opa, were the most down to earth people despite their wealth, and I loved them very much. Once they saw the welts and bruises on my backside, and became very upset, I believe they gave my mother a good talking to. But they were the ones who had spoiled her all their life.

Oma and Opa also had three sons. Uncle Erwin, the eldest, whom I didn't know very well, he was married and lived a distance away. Uncle Richard, who was supposed to take the estate over and lived at home, was my favourite. Uncle Arno, the youngest, was away at the university in Koenigsberg, and of course we spent a lot of time together at my grandparents during school vacations. He was like a big brother as he was only eleven years my senior. I shall return to my grandparents place later, as I spent the last years of my childhood and innocence there, but in the meantime, a lot of fateful events took place in the rest of Europe which affected my whole future.

In March 1939 Hitler announced the reunification of the 'Memelland' with Germany, which had been given to Lithuania in the Versailles Treaty in 1918. Hitler came to Tilsit and there were parades and flags everywhere. Everything happened right in front of our house on the Fletcher Plaza. The border guards were removed on both sides of the Queen Louise Bridge. Hitler made one of his, by now, predictable speeches, "Ein Volk—Ein Reich—Ein Fuehrer", meaning "One people—one empire—one leader." All German speaking people must live in one German country, etc., etc. I found his voice annoying and even as a young boy I thought there was something sinister about this man. Little did I, or anybody around me, know at that time that the most horrific war in the history of mankind was only six months away.

On this day I was only interested to walk across that bridge, which was approximately one mile in length, into what used to be Lithuania, for some fancy ice cream and whipped cream, which was a specialty there. Of course there was no school that day due to all the hoopla, so some of my school buddies and I did just that.

When I returned a surprise awaited me. My uncle Arno had arrived with his young bride. No one in our family, including my mother, knew that he got hitched. The wedding had taken place in Saarbrucken, Saarland, which had also been annexed by Hitler in 1936. The Saarland had been part of France after World War I. Uncle Arno's bride was beautiful, part French, and was the daughter of an industrialist. I think my mother was a little jealous, as Renee was dressed in the latest French fashion, and was, of course, about fifteen years younger than my mother.

Anyway, I walked into the living room, and there they were. I smartly gave them the Nazi salute. That is when my uncle Arno got up and slapped me, not hard, and he said, "In our family we shake hands, hug and kiss, none of this Hitler stuff. Now come and meet your aunt Renee and give her a kiss. She has come half way across the world to meet the rest of my family". In those days to travel from the French border to almost the Russian border, seemed to be half way around the world.

Little did I know that I would never see Uncle Arno again, that fall he enlisted in the navy and was made chief engineer on a submarine. He had taken engineering at the Koenigsberg University. In May 1940 our family was informed that my uncle Arno had been lost in action. My grandparents were devastated. He was only twenty-two and was their youngest. A year or so later, I found a letter that aunt Renee had written to my mother, bemoaning the fact that she was childless, if she had known, she would have preserved some of uncle Arno's sperm to become artificially inseminated. Of course, I didn't have a clue what she was talking about, and I didn't dare to ask my mother.

After the war, when I lived in Koeln (Cologne) which is not that far from Saarbrucken, I tried unsuccessfully to find Aunt Renee. As Saarbrucken was also very much destroyed, who knows what happened.

That summer, when school was out, my parents put me on a steamboat that regularly travelled the Memel river to the Baltic Sea, to spend my summer vacation with Oma and Opa, as I did every year. This was the first time I travelled alone I was only eight years old. In previous years, we always used our car it was only a two hour drive, by ship it took the best part of the day as it stopped numerous times. Actually, I was overjoyed to be away from my parents, and looked forward to spending two months on the farm with Oma and Opa, play with the labourers' children, run barefoot through the fields, and ride my favourite horse. Whether I was dreaming, or had fallen asleep, I don't remember, but I had missed my destination, and the captain had forgotten to remind me where to get off.

It was dark when we arrived at the ship's final stop. The captain told me to stay, I could bunk with one of the cabin boys, and he was going to make sure that I wouldn't miss my town on the return trip, which started at four A.M. the next morning. I wasn't worried, but wondered what my grandparents were thinking. I knew my mother had phoned them that I was coming. I ate with the crew and that night I cuddled up to the cabin boy, who was about sixteen, and I felt very secure. The water softly lapped at the ship and made it roll slightly and that made me feel comfortable.

The next morning the captain dropped me off at my destination and I walked the two miles of country road to my grandparent's farm. I knew most of the land along the way as most of it belonged to Opa. As a matter of fact, some of his land bordered on the river, and many a time I had climbed the dam and sat there to watch the ships and barges go by. All the land in that area is below sea level and therefore was protected by the dam, very similar to Holland.

When I arrived at my grandparents, they were worried out of their minds, and had made numerous phone calls. Oma was mad at my mother for letting me travel alone. Soon I settled in to a daily routine, although during a two month vacation there was always something new, something to explore.

The yard and its surroundings were very typical of that of a well established, well-to-do eastern European estate, centuries old. All buildings were arranged in a circle. There were two roads that led in and out of the property. The gates were guarded by two concrete lions sitting atop a twelve to fifteen foot column. A huge six hundred year old elm tree shaded the centre of the yard with benches and flowerbeds surrounding the tree. A driveway circled that little island of tranquillity.

The buildings surrounding the outside of the driveway consisted of the family house and next was a building that housed wagons, sleighs, uncle Richard's car and a mill with a tower that had a bell on it. Next was the horse barn with thirty stalls and six foaling compartments. There was also a bunk room for two horsemen. Attached to the barn was a shed for hay and straw.

The horses were Opa's pride. The breed was Trakehner, a breed named after Trakehnen, a town in East Prussia. They are a dual purpose horse, warm blooded, about sixteen hands tall, elegant and excellent for both riding and work. They are similar to the Hanoverian but are almost extinct now. There is presently a breeder who is trying to raise Trakehner in the western part of Germany. Opa sold studs and breeding stock all over Europe.

Next was the largest building which sheltered the harvest of rye, wheat, barley and oats. In the fall all fields were harvested with binders, pulled by tractors before the war, and by horses during the war as there was no fuel available. Private vehicles also could not be driven due to the shortage of fuel. During the war the wheels had to be taken off and the cars set on blocks. At harvest time all the bundles of grain were set up, nine per stook. After a few days all the bundles were loaded on wagons and driven home. They were unloaded in this huge storage building and stacked to the rafters. The building had eight bays and in the winter, the thrashing machine moved from bay to bay to thrash the grain. The straw was taken to the various barns to be used for bedding for the animals. All the hay was stored on top of the dairy barn and in a shelter at the horse barn.

The dairy barn housed eighty milk cows which were all registered Holstein. There were also several loafer compartments, open areas for heifers and calves.

Another building within the farm yard circle was the hog barn which housed three hundred pigs from farrowing to slaughter. I would like to point out that in the winter, unlike in Canada, not one of the farm animals was outside. Only in the summer were they pastured. Other buildings along the yard exit included machine shops, chicken and geese barns.

Along the entrance to the farm were four houses, each one occupied by two families who did all the chores on the farm. These workers and their forefathers had been with our family for generations. Each family owned a parcel of land, some chickens, one or two milk cows, and of course, earned their wages. The men did all the field work and fed the animals. The women milked the cows each morning starting at four A.M. and in the evening starting at four P.M. Each woman milked eight to ten cows, all by hand. During the summer, the milking was done in the pasture and in the winter, it was done in the barn.

All the manure from the animals was piled up on the outside of the barns, never inside the yard. Ever so often the manure was taken to the fields. It was loaded by hand with forks, then unloaded and spread, all manual labour. All the fields would be ploughed and fertilized with real manure, no chemicals whatsoever.

The house was approximately four hundred years old, built in the days of aristocrats and very well to do landowners. It featured rooms that were called the ballroom, the music room, the ladies' sitting room, the men's smoking room, the library, etc. The walls of the structure were about two feet thick and each window had an alcove. Each room was equipped with a stove that was six feet tall and covered with decorative tiles to match the decor of each room. These stoves were heated with huge bundles of sticks and branches from pruned trees that were collected during the summer by the young boys of the labourer's families. We had a beautiful forest and park, as well all the roads were lined with trees.

The main kitchen was dominated by an oven that was about eight feet long and six feet wide. Each week Oma and the maids were involved in baking bread for the family and the farm help. The bread was sourdough and rye. The dough was kneaded in a huge wooden trough, then formed into round shapes, the size of bicycle wheels and baked in that great, pre-heated oven. To this day, I can still smell and taste the fresh baked rye bread with homemade butter and Tilsit cheese.

My bedroom was upstairs, overlooking the flower garden with its pathways, benches, and hideaways surrounded by flowering shrubs, such as, lilac, snowball and jasmine. Next to the flower garden was a one acre parcel with apple, plum and sour cherry trees and numerous bushes of black, yellow and red currants, raspberries and gooseberries. On the outside of this was the vegetable garden. All the vegetables and fruit was made into preserves, canned and stored for the long winter. The huge cellar was filled with stone vats and crocks full of pickles vegetables, sauerkraut and other preserves. We also had a smokehouse, as we did all our own butchering and made all our own sausages, smoked hams and bacon.

As the reader may notice, I have switched to 'we', that is because my grandparents were my real loving and protective family and I was their son. Not only did we lose uncle Arno, but the following year in 1941 when Hitler invaded Russia, uncle Erwin and uncle Richard, who was to inherit the farm, were both "lost in action" within three months of each other. To this day I cannot fathom how my Oma and Opa coped with the pain of losing their three sons.

From now on, whenever I spent my vacations out there, they heaped all their love and affection on me. Opa taught me from an early age what there is to know about farming and animal husbandry. He taught me to respect the land and the animals. He also showed me, by example, to treat our labourers and their families as equals, with honesty and integrity. I learned how to help a cow calf, and had to pull a little piglet out of the mother sow as it had become stuck in her hip bones.

My grandfather was called "Der alte Herr", "the old gent" by everyone. He was loved and very much respected. In 1940 he was seventy years old, and very active, more so when his heir, Uncle Richard, went to war and did not return. So he started to groom me for the job, little did we know then what lay ahead of us. During World War I Opa was an officer in Kaiser Wilhelm's Cavalry. We had a huge picture of him in uniform on horseback that hung in the living room. He was very proud of his handlebar moustache which he preened and twisted and every night he wore protective elastic over that moustache.

How I miss this man, even today and how I miss Oma, and our Hohenwiese (high meadow) which was the name of the estate. To this day I can see every tree, pathway, faces of the people on the farm. I have tears in my eyes while I write this. Many nights I wake up, my pillow wet with tears from the dreams I had about the only truly happy times in my life. Before I die, I would like to once more walk through those gates into the farmyard, through the garden and the house. I would like nothing better than to die there and be buried in that little family cemetery in the pasture, under the shade of those elm trees. In that cemetery are the graves of my forefathers, dating back to the 16th Century.

Why dream? Who knows, there may be nothing left of the place. While we were on the run from the Russians in the winter of 1944–1945, we heard rumours that the German troops broke all the dams, and flooded the land before they retreated. Until one year ago, it was impossible to travel into that part of Russia. However, let's get back to Tilsit and school.

That fall I started my last year of elementary school, the following year, I would enrol in a high school for boys. The German school system at that time was such that if your future was that of labourer, you went to elementary school from age six to fourteen. If you wanted to become a tradesman or journeyman, you went to elementary school from age six to fourteen, then to middle school and apprenticed by age eighteen. If university was your goal, as was decided for me by my parents, you went to elementary school from age six to ten, then to "Oberschule", high school from age ten to eighteen, and then on to university. Students started learning English at age ten in high school, and then French and Latin at age fourteen.

One month after returning to school in 1939, Hitler invaded Poland. The propaganda machinery worked over-time to convince the German population, and the rest of the world that this became necessary because of alleged atrocities that the Poles were committing against Germans living in Poland. History is repeating itself today. Of course, Hitler's war machinery was so superior to any-thing Poland had to offer, that the country was completely occupied within three weeks. A new word was coined, "Blitzkrieg". Polish prisoners of war had the choice to either go to prison camps or work on German farms, as all the young men in Germany had been drafted and there was a large labour shortage.

England and France declared war on Germany but were too late to help Poland. Hitler and Stalin had a non-aggression treaty, so Hitler concentrated his forces on the western front. As a matter of fact, Russia occupied parts of Poland as well. By May 1940, all of Europe was engulfed in war. Hitler marched into France through Luxembourg, Belgium and Holland, in order to bypass the Maginot Line, the bulwark France had built along their eastern border. Of course, we in East Prussia were so far away from all this, and felt pretty safe from the ravages of war. France was completely occupied within six weeks and the British troops driven back to England.

Everyone, including Churchill was holding their breath, expecting the Germans to invade England, the United States had not entered the war yet, and England was at Hitler's mercy. No one knows for sure why this did not happen, there are many theories. The most popular one was that Hitler, who was fanatical about the purity and superiority of the Germanic race, believed that the world should be dominated by this race, and England was part of that race. Here is a man, an Austrian with black hair and brown eyes, whose Germanic background is very questionable, advocating this monstrous philosophy.

Nuts…I personally believe that Hitler, after having defeated France and feeling very safe as far as the western front was concerned, had his mind set already on Russia. Remember, the U.S.A. had not entered the war and most likely would not, if Pearl Harbour did not happen. The sentiment in America was to stay out of it. For centuries the Germans have used the cry for "Lebensraum" as an excuse to invade other countries, "Lebensraum" meaning living space. Western Germany was heavily populated, some two hundred people per square mile. Eastern Europe had lots of space and land available. The Baltic countries, parts of Poland, White Russia, and even the Balkans had a very large German population for centuries. That is why Hitler set his sight on Russia and because he feared Stalin, the Bolsheviks and communism. He felt that he could free armies from the western front and move them to the east. By 1941 the German military lines stretched from the Arctic Circle in the most northern part of Norway to Spain, and also occupied all of northern Africa, with the exception of Egypt.

So, despite the nonaggression pact with the Soviet Union German troops invaded Russia in June 1941 with a force and military power, the world had not seen. In Tilsit we awoke to the detonation of bombs and artillery at 4 a.m. June 22. The buildings were shaking, and we run outside in our nightgowns, and watched the light display in the sky. Air attack sirens had not been activated to this point, and air raid shelters were not operational.

The sounds of war only lasted three four days, and became more distant all the time, as the German troops advanced into Russia rapidly.

The day after the first bombs fell on Tilsit my mother packed me up, and moved me to my grandparents, summer vacation was only a few days away anyhow.

Everything was different,—Uncle Richard was gone, Opa, now seventy one years old, had to look after the whole operation again. All the young male farmhands had been enlisted, that included the men of the permanent labour families. The tractors were silent all the fieldwork had to be done with horses.

We had now six polish POWs on the farm, all in their early twenties. Muchinsky was a carpenter by trade, Michalsky was a butcher, Wandalin a university student, the other three, Stachek, Zigmond, and Kowalsky, had now trade I knew of. From the beginning I befriended Stachek and he spent a lot of time with me, we wrestled with each other and did a lot of fooling around. He was like a big brother and very protective of me. Stachek also taught me many polish words, most of which you could not repeat in front of ladies. I still remember most of them.

Opa gave them a very large room in an unoccupied building, which had six bunk beds in it, a table, chairs, and a stove. All their meals were taken in the kitchen, with the rest of the farm help.

Opa was supposed to lock their quarters at night, which he never did, as a matter of fact Zigmond had a Polish girlfriend at one of the neighbour's farm, two miles away whom he visited almost nightly. He took quite a bit of teasing as he seemed to be tired all the time. All six stayed with us over three years, eventually changed their status to that of civilian, and fled with us when the Russian armies approached.

During that summer I learned to milk, and every evening I milked # 60, named Orchid, which was my pet cow. All cows had horns, with a number branded into them. In the barn each cow had a tablet hung above their stand, which indicated the cows registered name, her age, the date she was due to calve and the name of the sire. I also had a pet sow, a St. Bernard dog, which pulled my sleigh in the winter, and of course my own horse, I loved to ride.

To this day I still love to drink milk fresh from the cow. I always kept a glass handy when milking. Often in the summer, when I was running barefoot through the pasture, I found Orchid, and stripped some milk right into my mouth.

In school I had read the story of Remus and Romulus, twin brothers who, as the legend goes, were raised by a female wolf, and later founded Rome. Curiosity got the better of me, and I wanted to put this story to a test,—since a wolf was not readily available, I went to the hog barn and laid down with my pet sow who happened to have piglets, and sucked on one of her teats. Lo and behold I managed to get some milk, it tasted kind of sweet. Was I a weird kid, or what? Anyway it proves that the Roman twins could have been raised by a she wolf.

That summer I also learned how to castrate little piglets. I did not particularly like it because I became upset with their squealing. Some sows were so agitated that they nearly jumped over the walls of their pen. Opa explained to me why it was necessary to castrate; however, I still wondered what if this was happening to me.

Although I had seen a lot of copulation among farm animals, which I watched with interest, at age ten I was extremely naïve about human sexuality. In those days most children about to reach puberty, did not have a clue what sex was all about. Oh the labourer children, and my friends at school, talked big, and even bragged about our knowledge of the subject, often we fooled around with each other, grabbed, touched and compared genitalia when swimming, skinny dipping in the river, I assume most boys go through this period, even today. However I believe that the behaviour of touching and grabbing is more common to East European countries than in other parts of the world.

One summer day, after loading hay in the field, Stachek and I stripped and jumped into the river. Not only was I awed by the size of his penis and testes, but also at all the pubic hair, I had never seen a full grown naked man or woman of course. Stachek told me not to worry, in a year or two I would look the same. I could hardly wait for that to happen.

In September I transferred to the Oberschule (High school) for boys. I was not an excellent student, although I could have been, but I did not enjoy to study. Learning and absorbing knowledge came easy. Although my parents locked me into my room for two hours each school day to study, I preferred to read books I hid books every where, at night I read under my bed covers by flash light. I enjoyed historical novels, about the Roman Empire, kings and emperors who had lived centuries ago. The subjects I excelled in were History, Geography, and Biology. I was average in Chemistry, Science and Geometry.

This was also the first year of learning English. It started out pretty good, however in November I came down with scarlet fever, which was very severe. My temperature was so high that I fell into a coma for days. Everyone feared for my life, but I was not ready to become an angel. The illness lasted six weeks, and I did not attend school for two months. This really set me back in my English, particularly English grammar. I was given the services of a tutor, to catch up to the rest of the class.

I always walked to school with one of my buddies who lived in my neighbourhood. We were the same age, he was of acceptable social standing in my mothers view, and therefore we could associate with each other.

It was a beautiful scenic walk to school, along a small lake with swans, geese and ducks. The swans occupied a little hut on an island, where they hatched their offspring. It was always an exciting time of the year, when the proud parents made their first appearance with the young. Even as a youngster I loved scenery and animals. As a boy, as well as today, I have raised many abandoned, hurt, or sick animals, mostly babies, to the point where they would be able to survive on their own. On most occasions I was successful. The animals ranged from piglets, calves, and foals, to owls, fawns and storks. The storks were quite a story.

Most farms in the area of my grandparent's estate had a stork nest on the rooftop of one of their buildings. The nest on our estate was located on the roof of the dairy barn. These black and white birds, with their long stilt-like red legs and long red beaks, knew the farms boundaries quite well they usually followed us when we ploughed the fields, caught frogs and worms while walking behind the plough. They returned from Africa each spring and took possession of their old nest. They announced their arrival by standing on the rooftop, raising and bowing their heads, while making a loud clapping sound with their long beaks. The same ceremony was repeated every time they returned from the field to feed their young. Each year the storks added to the structure of the nest. The one on our dairy barn was approximately two meters tall and weighed about a ton. One day the two young storks and the nest came tumbling down, and for some reason the parent storks would no longer look after them. I would not want storks like that deliver babies to my house. So it became my chore to raise these storks during that summer. They became quite aggressive and attacked me if I did not have any food for them.

During the spring of 1942 I noticed a boy who walked to school along the same paths that my buddy and I used. We noticed that this boy always walked alone, did not talk or associate with anybody and never made eye contact with us. Then we saw the yellow star on his jacket and the word "Jude" printed on it, which translates into Jew. The star of course was the Star of David. He was the only boy in my school identified as a Jew. At that time I was not aware that it was mandatory for Jews to be identified in this manner. That he was the only boy wearing the Star of David indicates to me that there were very few Jewish people in East Prussia, which was not the case on the German mainland. On radio and film we heard and saw a lot of propaganda against Jews, how they were out to undermine the goals of Hitler, and destroy the structure and the future of the Third Reich.

With shame I admit that all the kids, including myself, teased this boy mercilessly, however he just endured all the barbs and verbal abuse, never answered, just walked along stoically. One day he was not there, and never came back. At that time it was not of concern to me, nobody questioned where he was, we assumed his family had moved away. I did not know about concentration camps and the Holocaust till after the war. Ever since I knew, I can see the lonely, slightly stooped over figure of this young boy walking along that path. To this day I feel very guilty and ashamed. There was a time after the war, when I worked in Luxembourg, and later after I immigrated to Canada, that I would not admit to being German, I was always Austrian, Swiss or Lithuanian. Today I feel that I must face up to the sins of my forefathers and try to do my part to prevent these monstrosities from happening again.

That summer before going to the farm, my mother took me to a resort on the "Kurische Nehrung" (no translation), a narrow strip of land which divides the "Haff" from the Baltic Sea and the mainland. The Haff is a body of water that is not salty. The Nehrung consists of sand dunes, pine forests and beautiful sandy beaches all along the Baltic Sea. Smoke huts where fishermen smoke freshly caught eel, flounder and other tasty fish, are scattered along the beach. The smell of these smoke huts is still with me and makes my mouth water. Moose roam the pine forests and wade into the waters of the Haff, they are not afraid of people, and quite often come to the vacationers cottages. This is also the area where Bernstein (Amber) is found. If there is such a place as god's country, this has to be it. Why this part of Eastern Europe has not been developed for tourism is beyond me. Many people lose out on experiencing the beauty and tranquillity of this part of the world. On that particular vacation my mother came very close of actually acting and being a mother. That was the only time in my young life we were close. Normally my parents took their vacations at the French Riviera, Italy or Spain, without me of course, although I much preferred being with Oma and Opa on the farm.

Christmas vacation I was at the farm again. There were three additions to the workforce, A Ukrainian young man about twenty years of age, Dmitri was his name, he came from a farm in Ukraine, and Opa put him in charge of the dairy. He was very good looking, and one of the milkmaids, Mrs. K. whose husband was in the war, took a shine to him and seduced him to become her lover, although she was twenty years his senior. Relationships between German nationals and foreigners were forbidden by law; however, everybody on the farm ignored it. They carried on with their love affair till the end, I actually saw them having sex in the hayloft, at that time I thought they were wrestling.

The other two were young Lithuanian civilian men, kind of lazy, and did not want to associate with anybody else. One day in their room they undressed, and tried to involve me in different sexual activities, for a little while I was curious and willing, but got quite scared when they became more aggressive, and ran. I never went to their room again. Today I would have classified them as being gay, although I dislike putting labels on anyone, or being labelled by others. Who knows, a year or two later, when I reached puberty and became quite raunchy, I may have participated.

The winter was always slaughter time, geese, chickens, hogs and beef. Although during the war each farmer was given a quota of how many animals they were allowed to butcher, Opa did not pay attention to that. All animals were counted each year, and the total numbers had to be submitted to the Government, somehow he always managed to miss some. He believed that everyone who worked should be well fed. Many farmers were reported to the Government by their disgruntled help, sometimes by their own relatives, and paid a heavy price or went to jail. Opa had very loyal people on the farm, foreigners and Germans alike always stood by his side. As I mentioned earlier, one of the Poles was a butcher by trade, and a good one, as we soon found out. Winter was his busy time he made sausages, cured and smoked meat, and made sure there was a good supply of meat all year round.

The women were busy butchering geese, three hundred in total. The breasts and thighs were smoked, what a treat. Today in Canada I travel some sixty miles in order to buy some smoked goose breast at a German deli in Edmonton. The main purpose to raise and butcher that many geese however, was to save the down and feathers for bedding. If you have never slept in a bed with down filled pillows and covers, you have not slept in heaven.

What I enjoyed most in the winters on the farm, were the sleigh rides into town. Two horses, their harnesses covered with bells, pulled the sleigh. It was the most comfortable ride anyone can imagine. The seats were covered with bison fur, the blankets were also supplied by various animals, you felt so warm and cozy as one would today in the most luxurious car. Mind you today animal rights activists would most likely have doused our sleigh with paint, for having used all those fur blankets. The snow was so deep, that the sleigh just glided through it without hitting any bumps. How I wished all children in the world could enjoy these experiences—how soon all these enjoyments would come to an end, and never return.

In December 1941, after the Japanese attack on Pearl Harbour, the United States of America entered the war. Bombings of German cities increased drastically all through 1942, every major city experienced severe and devastating air raids. Quite often, one attack just being completed, the air raid sirens wailed again, preparing the civilian population for the next wave of bombings. This went on relentlessly, night after night. The skies lit up by burning cities. Places like Cologne, Hamburg, Munich and most industrial centres like Essen, Dortmund, etc. were finally reduced to rubble. It took its toll on the civilian population, not just in the loss of life—millions of civilians were killed—but also in a psychological sense. The elderly, the frail and children were deprived of their sleep and much needed rest. People quite often found their properties destroyed or damaged, when they left the air raid shelters. Thousands left the cities and escaped to the country side, if they could, and if relatives or friends would give them sanctuary. They were not always welcome by country folks. There was a lack of food, medical supplies and daily necessities. Many hospitals and schools were destroyed during these bombings.

During that period of the war, we in the East were not yet affected by the carnage that took place in the West, North and South of Germany.

That year I finally reached puberty, although I did not really know it. I had viewed myself in the mirror for months, to see if I could detect any pubic hair at all. When I noticed some downy fluff around my privates, I could hardly wait for my Christmas vacation to tell Stachek that his predictions had come true, and I was going to look like him in certain areas. One day I was sitting in the bathtub, exploring the lower extremities of my body, when all of a sudden I had this tingling sensation, and some clear fluid ejaculated from my erect penis. I became very scared, and would have run to my mother, if fear and shame would not have kept me from doing so. That shows how naïve I still was, today's kids would most likely laugh at me for being so ignorant of my sexual development. The boys in school talked about masturbation, and things like that, however I did not really know how it was done, and certainly orgasmic experiences were foreign to me. I believe that pre-teens and teens are very fortunate today to have sex education in school, and often from their parents.

Even though that first experience scared me, but natural urges took over, and it had felt kind of nice, that I kept on experimenting and exploring several times day and nights without any harm. Fortunately I had not heard the old tale of going blind.

That winter marked the beginning of the end, even though we did not know it yet. German troops had occupied most of the European part of Russia, and had by-passed Moscow. Now they were facing the same fate that befell Napoleon's army in 1812, the harsh Russian winter.

Stalingrad became the catalyst that marked the end of the early German successes. The results of the fierce battle at Stalingrad were both devastating and catastrophic. In the bitter cold winter conditions, after six weeks of the fiercest battle the world had seen, and more casualties on both sides than in any other war, the entire German sixth army was eventually surrounded and demolished. Most soldiers rather died than being shipped to Siberia. Also they were not allowed to flee or retreat, as Hitler had ordered any soldier who fled the battle field shot by the storm troopers (Waffen SS). Many people do not realize that there was a distinction between the ordinary German soldiers and the Waffen SS. They were the ones who came in after the battles were fought, they were the ones who committed most atrocities in occupied areas, they were the ones who rounded people up and shipped them to concentration camps. They were also hated and despised by the ordinary German soldier.

After Stalingrad the whole Eastern front was in chaos, the Germans retreated and the Soviets advanced rapidly toward Germany. We, in East Prussia would be the first ones to be attacked.

In June 1944 all healthy young boys twelve to fifteen.in age had to report to the Hitler Youth offices to be registered. We were shipped by boat along the Memel River into Lithuania to dig ditches and dugouts for the retreating German troops. Any young boy over twelve and older men over forty five, were enlisted already in the "Volksfront" Peoples Defence, to make a final stand and defend their homeland. I was twelve, big for my age, and was asked to join the several hundred who departed for Lithuania. My mother acted as if I was going to a picnic. Father had recovered quite well from his stroke two years earlier, but still was not healthy enough to enlist.

This was the most disorganized expedition ever put together, even I could see that. We dug ditches at random, there were no plans. Food supplies ran short after a few days. There was a shortage of tents or blankets to accommodate everybody. Many of us doubled up under one blanket on the bare ground. Fights broke out over food, sleeping arrangements and work assignments. Nobody knew who was in charge. The Lithuanians did not like us and would not give us food. They dumped soap into our well so we had no drinking water, and had to use water from a slough and from ditches. Many boys, myself included, suffered from diarrhea.

After three weeks of this the decision was made to ship us back home, and not too soon. We could hear the artillery and other noises of war in the distance. When I got home, my mothers only comment was, oh you lost weight. No hug, no affection, no question how it had been. Not only did I lose a lot of weight, my baby fat had all disappeared, but I had matured and felt much older than my twelve years.

The bombing of Tilsit had begun, and we spent most nights in the air raid shelters. I usually ventured outside to look at the light display in the sky. Some of the flares looked like Christmas trees above us. It was scary and fascinating at the same time. Being outside was better than sitting in the shelter, being thrown back and forth when the bombs exploded nearby, and listening to the whimpers and cries of old people and children. Many were praying as well.

In June my school was hit by bombs, even though this was close to summer vacation, I knew already there would be no school come September. My mother crated all valuables, including her Rosenthal china, family silverware, expensive paintings, etc. but she kept all her jewellery. All these crates, including a large case of old French Cognac, were taken to the steamship. I accompanied these riches to

Oma and Opa's farm. Mother had phoned them to meet me with a wagon and some help at the dock. Little did I know that this was the last time I would see my parents, or the city of Tilsit. I was elated to go to the farm, my real home, to people I loved, and who loved me.

Stachek was at the dock with a wagon and a team of horses to meet me. He had insisted that Opa sent him to pick me up. I was really happy to see him and he also had learned quite a few words of German, not only dirty words. The next few nights we were busy burying all the crates in different locations in the garden, just Opa, Stachek and myself. Sixty years later I cannot help but wonder if anyone ever found those treasures, or if they are still there,—we buried them quite deep in the ground.

In September 1944 German troops moved in, we accommodated some sixty military trucks and about two hundred soldiers and officers. They made themselves right at home. For the next three month we lived under some pretty crowded conditions, no privacy whatsoever. I made friends with a young soldier, George, he was from Bavaria. Quite often the two of us sat in his truck, and he told me about the mountains, skiing, the Oktoberfest in Munich, and of course of his conquest of girls. He could not get over all the flat land in East Prussia, and was amazed at the wide expense and open space all around us. He asked me to introduce him to a girl he had seen, she was the daughter of one of our labourers. It was hard on these guys, as there were only a limited number of young girls, and most of them made themselves available to officers only. I made the arrangement for George; however, the girl insisted that I sit in the truck with them. So I had to watch all the petting and kissing, pretending I was not there. Of course I became aroused, I am only human. On one of these occasions I believe they actually did it, the girl was sitting on his lap, moving up and down, the breathing getting heavier, then finally a big sigh from George,—that must have been it,—I think.

There was one incident during this time, that is worthwhile mentioning. The previous year one of our Holstein cows gave birth to a red and white calf, which created a sensation. None of us had ever seen a red and white cow or calf, not even my grandfather. This must have been a fluke and a throwback in pure Holstein breeding. Neighbours came from far and wide to have a look at this phenomenon. Needless to say it became my very special pet, and followed me around where ever I went.

This calf was a little more than one year old now, and one day two soldiers roped it, in order to butcher the poor thing. This upset me immensely and I asked them to let the calf go. They just laughed at me asking "What is the big fuss, we have been butchering all the time without interference from anyone." I was amazed at my anger and bravery, yelling at them, insulting them, and becoming more agitated by the minute. I finally grabbed a horse whip and whipped both soldiers as hard as I could, people gathered around, encouraging me to further violence, finally an officer stepped in to stop this nonsense. He actually apologized on behalf of the soldiers and instructed them to always ask permission from Opa whenever they intended to butcher one of our animals. Today I think that calf would have been better of to be butchered, when I witnessed the suffering of all farm animals over the next few month.

Now we heard artillery and gunfire all day and all night, and it was getting closer with each passing day.

Refugees started to arrive with wagons and on foot, some stayed a few days others moved right on. They told horror stories of how the Bolsheviks raped and killed young girls, women and even grandmothers. It was open season on anybody. To them Germans were there to be used, abused and killed, slaughtered like animals. A fourteen year old girl had been gang raped by more than thirty Bolshevik soldiers, then left there to die.

Soviet forces were under instructions from Stalin not to spare any German men, women, or children. Stalin and Hitler were both mass murderers, the likes the world had never seen, and hopefully will never see again.

Winter came with a vengeance in late October 1944. The first week in November we were told by the German military command, that we had to leave within three days, and that was an order. Not that anyone wanted to stay behind to be exposed to the horror and inhumane atrocities committed by the Bolsheviks. This was certainly a much more cruel and inhumane war than the First World War. Oma told me about her experiences during that time. Opa was away in the army, one evening while milking, Russian soldiers appeared at the barn door, asked for some milk, thanked her, and left. What a difference that was a war fought between countries headed by royalty and parliaments, not a war that was all about ideologies, Aryan supremacy and ethnic cleansing.

So we started packing, loaded four wagons with food, blankets and clothing, covered everything with tarps and selected eight of the most dependable Trakehner horses to pull the wagons. Young girls dressed in boys clothing and cut their hair, women made themselves look old and generally unattractive. Although we were told that this was only a temporary measure, soon the Russian armies would be defeated by the deployment of so called secret weapons, and we would be able to return, nobody believed it.

Our Polish friends, as well as Dmitri, decided to leave with us, they did not want to fall into Russian hands. Stachek always watched out for me, he was also Opa's most trusted help.

November 7th 1944 is etched in my mind as the saddest day in my life, that is the day I lost my roots, my home, my safe haven, to me the most beautiful place in the world, —Hohenwiese. For the rest of my life I would search for a place I could call home. Yet I never succeeded. Later on in my life I would purchase and sell many properties, even tried to recreate the old estate, but could not. Sixty years later I can see every tree, building, and bend in the road, and no matter how successful I became in later years, it was never home. Even at my advanced age, I often wake up at night, my pillows wet from tears shed during a vivid dream of my home. History had written a new chapter.

We joined the thousands of wagons on the road, one that led to many great sufferings, hardships, and many deaths. The great trek reportedly involved more than twelve million people from various eastern countries. Some four million are still not accounted for.

So my childhood, troubled in many ways, but also carefree and happy during vacations and other occasions had come to an abrupt and unexpected end. Over the next four years events forced me to grow up fast. I would never experience the joys and fun times of being an adolescent or teen.

The next few years would shape and develop the man I am today. I may have stumbled a few times along the way, but I was always able to form my own opinions and to live by principle, setting high standards for myself and those around me, particularly those who wanted to be my friends.

3

The Trek

My dictionary tells me that TREK means a slow and arduous journey by wagon, what it does not say, that it means a journey through hell.

Our group of four wagons included forty one people, Oma (age 60), Opa (age 74), the six poles, Dmitri, the eight wives of the labour families, their twenty three children, ages 3 to 15, and myself age 12.

The German troops stayed behind of course and told us not to worry, they would drive the Ruskies back to Mongolia, and we would find everything the way it was when we left, yeah. Before we left, we opened all the barn doors and let all animals run out, as did most of the farmers. It was an unforgettable sight the sound of frightened and suffering animals were heart wrenching. These poor creatures had never been outside in winter conditions. The temperature was around minus twenty five Celsius. In December and January it dropped to minus thirty five. Cows were bellowing, their udders bursting, the horses left behind, ran after us. My red and white heifer came running up to me and licked my clothing. I just broke down and I suddenly realized that I would never see home again. I threw myself in the snow, tears streaming down my face, I looked up toward heaven, Still believing in a god who saw everything, forgave our past sins and loved all his children, I cried out to him, why, why,—but he would not hear me, and I did not know the answer. All I knew was this was madness. Stachek came over, picked me up, and tried to console me, without success.

The first day we travelled about twenty kilometres. Oma and Opa rode in the wagons, heavily bundled up. They did not show any emotions, even though their life had come to an end, they knew there was no future for them. They had lost three sons while defending the fatherland. Their home and estate that had been in the family for seven hundred years was gone forever, and why, because of one madman wanting to rule the world. Yet we are still to believe in a loving god.

The rest of us walked. We kept to secondary roads to avoid the military and armoured vehicles. The plan was to cross the "Haff" which would have been a shortcut, and make it to Danzig (Gdansk) in Western Prussia, where we hoped to board a ship to cross the Baltic Sea. The Haff froze every winter, and it was normally safe to drive on the ice. Danzig was about five hundred kilometres. At twenty km per day, it would take about twenty five days to reach our destination. Oma had talked to my parents by phone before we left. They were to leave Tilsit when the evacuation orders came, and meet us in Danzig. These plans however never materialized.

At night we camped in farmyards, and slept in barns and haylofts. Some of the farms were abandoned already, on others the people were packing and ready to leave. There were those who put up a brave front, and said they would rather die than leave their home. We encountered some good old folks who would not let us spend a night on their property, and treated us with open disdain and hostility. It is in times like this that one may lose faith in the human race.

Usually the men slept together in the haylofts, and so did the women. Opa and I always slept under the same blanket, trying to keep each other warm. My Love for this proud old man was overwhelming. As I am writing this, approaching the age he was then, I cannot help but pause once in a while, as the water in my eyes blurs my vision. This is almost sixty years later, and I still love him.

During all this chaos and hopelessness, I could see that life would always go on. I realized this when all of us could hear young Dmitri and Mrs. K. engage in sexual activities at night, caring not who could hear.

A few days later we found out that the route across the Haff was no longer feasible. We met some refugees who had seen hundreds of wagons break through the ice and just disappear. So we changed course, rather than heading west, we continued moving south toward Elbing (Eblag) and west from there.

The days were getting colder, and a biting east wind was with us all the time.

We came across frozen dead bodies in the ditches, older people who had succumbed to the cold and new born babies who never stood a chance. Maybe they were better of. One day I saw a dog chew on the body of a dead baby, I puked my guts out. Would I ever grow up to be a normal human being? We did not have the services of Social Workers and Psychiatrists during those chaotic times. The count of the dead mounted, as we were now harassed by Russian fighter plane pilots, who made machine gunning people, horses and wagons, a sport, lots of fun to them.

We were now on the road for one month, it was mid December, food was running short and it was getting to be bitter cold. We decided to load all our belongings and remaining food on two wagons, which left two horses idle. Eventually they were butchered to keep us in food. By Christmas we had reached

Preussisch Eylau, a small city in West Prussia. Christmas was not on any ones mind. How could we even think about this holiday that was celebrated in Germany as nowhere else in the world? Surrounded by death, hunger, sickness and destruction, not even the birth of our saviour could bring us hope.

Opa was very sick with typhoid fever, brought on by drinking contaminated water, and possibly food that had gone bad. In my opinion he simply lost his will to live, having lost everything, including his three sons, and now watching his pride and joy, the Trakehner horses, being butchered. His health deteriorated fast. Two days after Christmas I awoke to feel his cold and lifeless body beside me. I had no tears, and there was an emptiness inside me that would not leave me for a long time. Deep inside me I thought it to be a blessing, how it must have hurt him not to be able to provide for those he loved. He would not have survived the hardship that was still to come. We buried Opa in the deep snow and moved on.

The following day our faithful Polish friends left us. We were now very close to their homeland, the part of the Province we were in now, used to be the Polish Corridor, and became a part of Poland again at the end of the war. We had come to a full circle, Hitler's pretext to invade Poland, was to eliminate the Corridor, and reunite East and West Prussia with the German mainland. Stachek and I said our "Goodbyes" and he took it harder than I did, as Opa's death had numbed me completely. While I am writing this, I hope that he is still alive, and through some miracle reads my story. He would be in his early eighties now.

More bad news followed, in January we were told not try to reach any Baltic port. The Russian troops had bypassed us to the north and the south, so we decided to press on straight west. Also one of the refugee ships, the "Gustloff", had been torpedoed. There had been two thousand people on board, all perished in the ice cold waters of the Baltic Sea. It is believed that my parents had been on this doomed ship. No award winning movie from this disaster.

By March we were within thirty kilometres of Dresden, the capital of Saxony, the city known as the Florence of the north, one of the most cultural centres of Europe, full of art museums and palaces, famous for Dresden china and figurines, sought after around the world. This city of six hundred thousand was the only metropolis of its size that had been spared allied bombings, due to the fact that there was no industry or military within its walls. There were however more than half a million refugees in the city.

Then one night it happened, American and British bombers attacked in three waves, each wave consisting of about five hundred planes. We watched it all from our camp. The sky was red from the burning city. The allies used phosphorus bombs to burn one of the most beautiful cities in the world to the ground, in the process killing some three hundred thousand civilians within a time span of ninety minutes. The next day we were told of people, engulfed in flames, throwing themselves into the Elbe River. Utter insanity. Can anyone keep track of the number of war crimes committed by the Allies? Yet the guilty were never taken before a war crimes tribunal after the war, neither were those that ordered the atom bombing of Hiroshima and Nagasaki. Lesson learned—when you are the victor, justice does not apply to you.

We moved on for another week on foot, each one carrying a pillowcase of our meagre belongings. The last two horses had been butchered a few days earlier. We arrived at a very small farming community called Aseleben, located on a lake. Oma and I were taken in by a very kind family, who owned the pub in that village. They had lost their only son in the war, and were still grieving. The husband was a communist, and could not wait for Hitler and his cronies to be defeated. He also was a very kind man. After four month of inhuman suffering, we had a bed to sleep in, had water to bathe in, clean drinking water and food. It is truly amazing how human beings will adapt to the most adverse circumstances.

Oma cleaned their house, did the cooking, and generally worked as a maid, in exchange for room and board. The rest of our group hired on as farm help with other towns people.

This was so different from where we had come from. These people, although they farmed, did not live on farms. They lived within the walls of a community, while their land was outside the town. Later I would see this system in other parts of Germany as well.

My childhood came to an abrupt halt when we were forced to leave home, however I shall end that chapter of my life at this point, when I wrongly assumed that we finally had reached a safe haven—wrong again.

4

Adolescent Years

Aseleben was a very small, picturesque and isolated community. The train station was about three kilometres away, so was the major highway. Were it not for families that had lost a husband, father or son, you could have sworn that five years of war had bypassed this town.

Oma insisted that I returned to school, it had been nine month since I had seen a classroom. The nearest college, equivalent to my school in Tilsit, was the Martin Luther College in Eisleben, a small city of approximately thirty thousand inhabitants, who had not seen any war activities either. This was April, 1945, in a few days I would turn thirteen. Anyone with eyes to see and ears to hear, knew the end of the war was near, in spite of the propaganda spewed out by Hitler and Dr. Goebels about secret weapons soon to be deployed. The allied troops were rapidly approaching from the west, encountering little resistance. The Russians were slowed down by fierce fighting in the east. It was a race who would enter Berlin first. Our landlord, who was a communist, hoped that Saxony would be occupied by the Russians, but he was an exception in that hope.

As I soon found out, it mattered not what nationality the approaching troops were, they all became involved in atrocities against mankind. In those days the hatred against anything German was overwhelming. As I found out after the war this hatred was warranted to a point. I am talking of course about the Holocaust and other crimes committed by the Nazis.

Even though, irregardless of anything I had seen and experienced during those horrible years, I would never be able to hate. All human beings are emotional creatures with certain traits and personalities, able to be kind and cruel, able to love or hate, compassionate and indifferent. Nationalities, creed and race are unimportant.

In order to go to school, I had to walk three kilometres to the train station every morning to catch a school train. It was a forty minute ride. I liked the school and the city of Eisleben it was very old and had a rich history, going back to the days of Martin Luther.

One day in mid April, American fighter planes attacked the train, even though it was identified as a school train by a red cross painted on top of the locomotive. First they planted two bombs in front of the engine to make the train stop. Hundreds of students spilled out in chaotic fashion, trying to take cover along the tracks. We tried to protect ourselves by covering our heads with schoolbook satchels. The fighter planes flew very low along the tracks, machine gunning the children as they passed over us, then they made a circle and returned for a second attack. The screams and cries of wounded and dying children would be embedded in my mind forever, much more than the sound of gun fire. When the planes returned for the second time, I threw all caution to the wind and looked up. I could see the pilots face, grinning, thoroughly enjoying himself. "Lets give those little Kraut bastards a lesson they will never forget", in anger and frustration I made a fist, and shook it at him. He was right about the point of never forgetting, that grinning face I would recognize even today. A little girl next to me had a leg shot of, she bled to death and I covered her with my jacket, thinking that she possibly saved my life. There were of course no ambulances or any help available. Finally some farmers arrived with wagons and horses, and the wounded children were loaded on one wagon, the dead on another. I walked back to Aseleben, about twelve kilometres, and had no desire to talk to anyone at that time. That was the end of school for two years. I do hope that the grinning pilot will live a long life filled with nightmares of those mutilated and dying children.

We were not the only refugees in Aseleben, in the house across the street from us, lived a mother with two daughters, they had been bombed out in Koeln (Cologne) the previous year, and had fled to Saxony to live with relatives. The girls were very pretty, redheads both. The younger one and I started to see each other, going for walks, holding hands, petting, etc. the first feeble attempt at puppy love. She was three years my senior, but we were attracted to each other. Oma became good friends with her mother.

Then one day toward the end of April, American soldiers drove into town and officially occupied it, there was no fighting whatsoever, we had not seen German troops for weeks. The Americans made our landlord mayor of the town, and for two days searched all houses officially for hidden Nazis and weapons. In reality, they were looking for valuables, in particular antiques that they could ship to the U.S.A.

About eight of them entered our house. The landlord was worried about his wine cellar, which was stocked with a fair amount of good vintage wine. He wanted me to talk to the soldiers, since I had learned a few basic sentences of English in school and could converse a little in that language. The lesson I was about to learn, was that of utter bewilderment, as well as physical pain. I walked up to one of the soldiers, took his hand, and shyly asked, "Will you take me to America I want to be your baby". First of all I said this to distract them from the wine cellar. Secondly, and most important, the word "Baby" to me meant child, therefore what I had asked, was if he would take me as his child. I had no idea that "Baby" was a synonym for sweetheart to Americans, in particular soldiers.

You can be my baby alright, he said, and winked at one of his buddies. They took me outside of town into a bush, and ordered me to take off all my clothing I was then raped by both. The pain was almost unbearable, but I did not cry out, I had tears in my eyes, more from humiliation than anything else. When finished, they took of in their jeep laughing. I must have lain there for an hour, completely numb. I could not think, as my mind was blank. I never talked about this until fifty years later at a native healing circle in Canada. That was the only time I let my guard down, and let my emotions take over. Up to that point I completely voided my brain of that occurrence it just never happened. Sex of that nature between two males, was completely foreign to me. Mutual masturbation and fooling around, I had known, but that seemed to be natural when growing up. Anyway after laying there for a lengthy time, I completely barred the incident from my mind, and walked home, pretending it never happened.

Two weeks later, the most inhumane war in history, was over. There were no celebrations or joy. I doubt if in all of Germany you could find one family that had not been touched by the ravages of war, in one way or another. Pending on the severity of the impact the war has had on each individual, we may heal fast, slowly or not for years to come—my scars will never heal. To the casual observer I may appear to be a happy well adjusted person, the reality is very different, deep inside me is a very sad and deeply hurt being, who even in his advanced years dreams the elusive dream of a perfect world, —UTOPIA.

For the next two years people in the cities had very little food. Hunger, malnutrition, and sickness were everywhere. The major cities were reduced to dust and rubble. People lived in cellars or bombed out buildings. The black market was thriving, young people survived by cheating, stealing or by prostituting themselves. With all the American, British, French and Russian occupation forces in Germany, prostitution was one of the easiest means of survival. Germany was divided in four Zones, the fourth being the French zone, De Gaulle had insisted that he would receive equal billing to the big three. The millions of German refugees were barely tolerated by the population, and very much discriminated against. We were foreigners in our own country. In Aseleben we did not experience that. I worked now on a farm hoeing beet fields all day long, there were seven workers in the field, all women, except me. I did get a very good sex education, verbally that is. It seems all these women could talk about was about their most intimate experiences with various soldiers, or their own husbands, who still had not returned home. I can assure you that women among themselves talk more about these subjects than men, although men usually take the rap.

There was a mentally challenged family in town, consisting of the parents and three adult siblings, two boys and one girl. They had all been sterilized under Hitler's law, and talked freely about it. The girl, now in her late teens, worked the fields with us. She told us quite proudly that a German officer picked her up when she was twelve. He took her to camp, where he proceeded to have sex with her, then passed her on to several of his soldiers. As I said she was very proud of this experience. I also remember that she wore no panties in the field, she hoed the row of beets ahead of me, and I could see her privates in all their glory. Of course I had never seen this on a grown woman before.

My girlfriend from across the street told me about dancing lessons commencing soon in the neighbour town. I was easily persuaded to go with her. The problem was that I did not possess a suit or slacks. So I took a pair of trousers from my landlord's closet, without him knowing. He was a huge man, weighing about two hundred fifty pounds, and sporting a big potbelly. I weighed about one hundred ten pounds, tall for my age and very skinny. I wrapped those trousers around me, tied them with a rope and pulled a sweater over the whole ensemble. I then snuck out of the house without being seen, and decked out like that we walked to the next town once a week to take up ballroom dancing. I must have been a sight. Although I was still only fourteen, I passed for sixteen. In my youth I always looked older than my true age.

In August the same year, the Americans left, and Russian troops moved in, that is when we became aware how Germany was to be divided in accordance with the Yalta agreement. Thuringia and Saxony which had been occupied by the Americans, was handed to the Russians. How the politicians in Washington came to regret that deal in future years. This was the beginning of communist East Germany, and the start of the cold war. Fortunately that also changed future American politics on the importance of a strong West Germany, as buffer against any communist aspirations to overrun Europe.

In accordance with the Morgenthau plan, all of Germany was supposed to become enslaved after the war, its industry never to be rebuilt again. Well that monstrous plan was quickly abandoned when the Americans realized that a strong West Germany would be a major catalyst in their fight against the east bloc. As a result the Morgenthau plan was scrapped, and the implementation of the Marshall plan began, which assured the miracle economic recovery of Germany. All that was still a few years away.

Oma was quite worried about Russians being our new masters, so was the family from Cologne. There was a rumour that a wall would be erected to separate the East from the West. In September Oma left with her friends by train, I was to follow once she was settled in Cologne. I behaved and acted like a twenty year old. The past two years had taken its toll and I had become very independent, wise, and mature far beyond my age.

A few weeks later I saw an ad in the paper, a bakery was recruiting an apprentice in a small town near Halle. The next day I rode my bicycle to that city, about twenty kilometres, and was accepted to apprentice. It was a father and son operation, the son had just returned from the military. Both their wives worked in the store selling all bakery goods. Of course everything was still rationed, but they operated a profitable business. Both, father and son were very strong Nazis. I shared a room with another apprentice who was in his third year, and had one more year left before he could take his journeyman exam. Man, how I despised the son who was my boss, and was very abusive physically. I truly believe he was a sadist by nature. For every little error he would slap or kick me, and I mean hard. He of course knew that I was alone, and could not complain to anyone. In those days there were no child protection agencies.

I got up every morning at four Am to make dough for bread and buns, at seven Am they were baked, I loved that smell. Part of my job was to deliver freshly baked goods to our regular customers, collected their ration stamps and money, and returned to the bakery. Delivery was done by bicycle that had a big basket in the front filled with fresh bread. I enjoyed that part of the job, as I met a lot of people. Some gave me tips, others however asked me to sell them bread at the black market price, for they were short on ration stamps. I felt sorry for some people, particularly if they had hungry children to feed, so I hid some loafs of bread in my bed to take out the next day, and hand it to these people during my delivery. The other apprentice must have seen me and informed my boss. He came and searched my room and that is when I received a severe beating. From then on he counted every loaf of bread before I left.

In the meantime I had met some people that were going to flee to West Germany by night. They had contacted a guide, who for a fee, would lead them through the so called "No mans land", a twenty kilometre strip of uninhabited land between East and West. I asked them to go along. The scheduled day I left for my regular delivery, but instead of collecting my customers ration stamps, I sold them the bread at twenty marks per loaf, which was cheap, considering it sold for sixty marks on the black market. One pound of sugar was eighty marks, butter and meat nobody could afford. So I became a criminal, but did not feel like one. Anyway I had enough money to pay the guide. I never went back to the bakery, and left the bike at the Halle train station where I boarded the train to Nordhausen, which was at the end of the track in East Germany.

That night I met with the group of refugees as prearranged. There were about twenty of us, all young people, and young families with children. That night we were ambushed by a group of robbers who demanded all our belongings. I only had the clothing I was dressed in. The little money I had was taped to my crotch. I still believe that our guide was involved in this profitable venture. By morning we were safely in West Germany and I boarded a train to Cologne, to finally meet up with Oma again.

Koeln (Cologne) was the largest city I had ever been to, population over one million. The well known Rhein (Rhine) river flowed through the city. Cologne of course was famous for its gothic cathedral, roman ruins and Eau de Cologne. The city itself was reduced to rubble, and ninety percent of it had been completely demolished along with Hamburg and Munich, and was the most severely bombed city in Germany. These bombardments took place relentlessly night after night, for a period of three years. Can anyone imagine the sufferings of the population during those years, apart from the millions that lost their lives?

And yet, amazingly people lived, loved, worked and fought with each other, as they had done for centuries. They also took advantage of the weak and down-trodden, nothing seemed to have changed—strange animals we are indeed.

Oma and the family she had accompanied to Cologne, lived in a bombed out house near the railroad tracks. She had one room with a cook stove, one table, one bed, and three chairs—that was it. The windows were broken. In the winter snow covered the floor. How she had survived so far, is beyond me. She was now sixty two. Oma had always been a heavy set woman, now she was quite frail.

I did get a job in a junkyard, sorting scrap metal, the pay was barely enough to cover the cost of bread, potatoes and soups; however it kept both of us alive. Most young people were busy on the black market, Hohe Strasse, which today is the high fashion street in Cologne, it was the black market hub and was illegal, but many made their living that way and became wealthy. I was not streetwise, and did not possess the shrewdness required to be successful in this racket.

Everybody in the building we lived in watched for freight trains carrying coal. As soon as a train approached, we jumped on to the track with sacks and pails, ran along the train and pried the doors open, and let the coal spill out. Everyone would take as much as they could carry. Oma was happy to have me around. I slept on the floor, rolled up in a blanket. We had a rule never to talk about Opa and Hohenwiese, but I could feel how she grieved and hurt inside.

I still chummed around with the young girl I originally met in Aseleben. She had developed into a beautiful young woman, eighteen years old, while I still was only fifteen. However I found it very difficult to relate to people my own age. My teen years were some of the most difficult and frustrating years of my life. Years that were supposed to be fun, experiencing the wonders of growing up, were completely lost. It was as if these years had passed me by. In the summer my girlfriend and I spent a lot of time on the beaches of the Rhine River, she turned many heads, and I was proud as a peacock. She also was very interested in classical music, and took me to my very first opera. The grand opera house was demolished, and the performance took place in the gymnasium of a school, that had survived the bombings. The production was Aida, and the place was packed. People had been deprived of any cultural events, they shouted so many "Bravos", and gave so many standing ovations to last the actors a lifetime. It was quite a sight, people in old raggedy attire attending an opera—what a difference from the lavish productions my parents used to attend in Tilsit. One thing was certain, people wanted to return to some resemblance of a normal life.

One morning that August I awoke to find Oma dead, she had succumbed to a massive heart attack. Now I was completely alone, I had not one living relative I was aware of.

I believe that the year of 1946 defined my future life. This was the crossroad, all the troubles I had seen, the loss of everyone I cherished and loved, abused and often beaten, hungry, cold and so very lonely, I could easily have taken the wrong path, heaven knows the opportunities were there. Many teens became involved in theft, robberies and sold the stolen goods on the black market. Other boys and girls my age sold their bodies to older men at the railroad station. I guess I was just not cut out to become involved in any of these activities. I took the hard road.

Although when I was hungry, I sometimes walked miles to the outskirts of the city, where people had gardens, and stole some vegetables and fruit, but I do not consider that criminal, my hunger had to be stilled somehow. One day I was so desperate that I filled a brown paper bag with salt, in order to sell it at the black market for sugar. If that was not the height of stupidity, of course the potential buyer tasted the "sugar" and chased me down the street, however I outran him.

On a wet and cold November day, I was alone in my room, shivering and hungry, so I decided that life was not worth living, worse than the hunger and cold, was my loneliness, my craving for love and understanding. I took a knife, a very dull knife, and commenced to cut my wrist, I was cutting back and forth with the dull blade, finally drawing some blood, when my former girlfriend walked in. I have neglected to mention that she had met someone else, and decided that I had no future. Anyway when she walked in and realized what I was trying to do, she became quite agitated, wrestled the knife from me and made me promise not to do this again. She was quite serious about the young man she was seeing, who happened to be a policeman. The next day I was introduced to him, and he asked if I would be willing to work on a farm. He had relatives in the country that could always use some help. I said anything is better than my present existence, and he bought a train ticket to my destination in the Eifel mountain region. It was on route from Cologne to Trier (Treves) on the Moselle River, a city older than Rome. The next day I left, and believe me I shed no tears.

When I arrived at my destination it was getting dark, although it was early in the evening. I was asking for direction to the little farming community, and was told that it was a five Km walk. So I started out on a dirt road that had become slushy from the melting snow. The soles on my shoes had holes in it, and soon my feet were wet and muddy, every step I took, it sounded like squish, squish. I was wet and hungry, my clothing tattered, the jacket I wore, was very thin, I had no other belongings, not even a toothbrush. When I finally arrived at the edge of town, I approached the first building I came to, everybody was busy doing their chores in the barn, and I asked where the people lived whose name I had written down. No problem, they gave me directions, this was a very small farming community, some three hundred people. There was a store, a blacksmith, and two pubs. Both pubs had a dancehall and a bowling alley. There was a church across the street from one of the pubs, which was very important as I later found out. This part of Germany was one hundred percent Roman Catholic, which somewhat influenced my life over the next few years. As usual I am getting way ahead of myself, as my mind is always racing.

When I met the people I was supposed to stay with, and work for, I felt very good about it all. This has become a trait with me, when I meet someone, the vibes are either good, bad, or indifferent, I strongly believe in first impressions. When I made the acquaintance of these people, my first impression was very positive. This became my permanent home for the next two years, and these new people, would be the nearest thing to a family for the next ten years, when I immigrated to Canada.

Right away they asked me to sit at the table and gave me something to eat. Food so delicious, I could not remember the last time it tasted so good. I had to force myself not to gulp it down. The family consisted of the parents and three sons, the oldest was one year younger than me, and I could wear some of his clothing. From the start they made me feel at home, and I became part of the family. Later I realized how hard these people had to work to make a living. Most farmers in those parts of the country were poor and every member of the family had to chip in to survive. I guess today they would be called dirt farmers, and I do not say that they are less than a farmer with a thousand acres of land. They just had to work much harder physically to make a living. All labour was performed manual, from raking hay to harvesting their crop in the fall. When I asked to see the horses, the older son replied "I show them to you." He took me to the barn which was attached to the house, which was a novelty to me. Pointing to four cows, he said "these are our horses." I thought he was joking, trying to test me to see if I could tell the difference between a cow and a horse. But he was serious and in weeks to come, I found that these Brown Swiss cows were providing milk, and were also used to pull a wagon, plough, and harrows. I also discovered that they were very slow and could be stubborn.

In the beginning I had a difficult time understanding the people in the community, as they spoke their own dialect, which I could not speak or understand. There are some forty dialects spoken in Germany, depending which part of the country you live in, although everyone understands "High German" which is taught in all schools across the country, at home people speak there own dialect. East Prussia had its own dialect, although my parents spoke "High German" only. I still can sing one song in the dialect of East Prussia. In time I mastered the Eifel dialect that is when I became part of the community. Peter, the oldest son was apprenticing in a butcher shop in the neighbouring town, while still going to school. His dad was making extra money by being the butcher for the whole community. He always brought fresh sausages and meat home. Every winter we butchered ourselves. All merchandise was still rationed, and very expensive, therefore all clothing for us boys was purchased with hams, sausages and meat.

Peter's dad treated me better than his own sons, he was a very tough acting man, rough on the outside, and mellow inside. He never talked much, but I soon realized his bark was much worse than his bite and he certainly was a very caring man. His wife was tiny, and a bitter woman, she resented her husband very much, although they had lived together and tolerated each other for sixteen years. I became her confidant, and several months later she told me that the troubles started on their wedding night. Being a very strictly raised Catholic girl, she had been a virgin when they married. That night, her new husband acted like a bull in heat and forced her to submit to his desire. Ever since, she disliked sex, and thought it was disgusting, but had to endure it to have children.

She and the boys were a united front against their father, to the point that they never addressed him, and he in turn only barked at his wife and the boys, often it became quite uncomfortable for me.

I didn't earn wages just pocket money, food, and clothing. Gradually I became involved in all kinds of activities. I started attending night classes to continue my education. Church on Sunday was a must, otherwise the girls were forbidden to dance with you at the dances every Sunday night.

Sunday's routine was, church in the morning, the women had to show off their new hats or other new attire, the men stood in the back, discussing the status of their crop, or my sow had ten piglets last night. After mass the women and children went to the cemetery next to the church, to say a prayer for those passed on, before they went home to prepare dinner. The men and older boys, age fourteen and up, went to the pub across the street, to play cards, or to bowl for beer. What is amazing, with all the drinking, even at a young age, I never met an alcoholic in any of these farming communities. I soon learned to bowl and play "Skat", a card game only played in Germany.

After dinner everyone went out to watch the local soccer game. Every small town had their own team. Soccer was the main organized sport in Germany, and in all of Europe. All the teams were involved in league play at different levels. I joined up and developed into a fairly good player. Sunday nights young and old went to one of the pubs to dance. The war was over and people tried to forget. I loved to dance and at the risk of sounding off, I was considered to be an excellent dancer, quite sought after by the girls. I also joined a theatre group, and the church choir. Each town competed against each other, in the winter it was theatre productions, and in the summer competitions among choirs, called music festivals. The competitions always took place on Sundays. Invited choirs performed during the day in huge tents. Theatre productions were usually held in the evenings in the dance halls, and were always followed by dances, which never ended before two Am. We walked to every town, and again home in the early morning hours. Nobody possessed a car, and distances between these towns could be as far as eight kilometres. We always walked in large groups singing as loud as we could. I believe that when people were able to purchase their own cars, and the availability of other transportation, community life, close knit friendships and camaraderie died.

The downside of all the fun was to milk cows at six a.m., and to do my chores. During the Mardi Gras, which is called Carnival or Fasching in Germany, we never went to bed at all for three days and nights. I really enjoyed those masquerade balls, and it was all clean and enjoyable fun.

Three of the farmers in town also operated a distillery, which was legal. All highways and roads in that area were lined with apple, plum, pear and sour cherry trees. Every fall the distillers bid on those trees, and hired the youth to pick the fruit. It was taken to their farms to be converted into Schnapps, highly potent, almost ninety percent proof alcohol. The residues were fed to the hogs and cattle. The custom was to go out and serenade these distillers on their birthdays, in gratitude we were given all the Schnapps we could drink and quite often could not handle. On one of these excursions I got so violently sick, from the alcohol of course, that I made the promise to myself "never again." I remember kneeling at a manure pile, trying to focus on some distant lights in a farmyard. Suddenly these lights started to dance around, faster and faster, my gut just exploded and I could not stop vomiting for over an hour. My buddies loaded me onto a wheelbarrow, which had been used to transport manure from the barn, and wheeled me home. My foster mother went into hysterics, she thought I was dying, I sure wanted to. Ever since that experience fifty six years ago, I have watched my alcohol intake. I always know when I have reached my limit.

At one of the Masquerade dances I met my future wife, although at that time I did not know this, as we did not get married for another fifteen years, long after I immigrated to Canada. At that time we just enjoyed each others company, we were both good dancers, and had lots of fun on many occasions. However she came from a well to do family in a neighbouring town, while I was just a poor refugee kid.

Once in a while some of us went to see a movie in one of the larger towns. One day I found out that they were showing "Die Reise nach Tilsit", (Journey to Tilsit), a film made before the war, a drama about a fisherman who intended to drown his wife in the Memel river on their weekend journey to Tilsit, because he had fallen in love with another woman, etc. I should have stayed away from that movie. When I saw the Queen Louise Bridge, and all the other familiar buildings, I started to tremble. My body was racked with uncontrollable sobs, and I had to run from the cinema. My friends could not understand what was happening to me, they did not realize that I just had a glimpse of what had once been.

I had quite a few friends, male and female, all of them older than me, and I felt much older than my actual age.

A few young men from our town had gone to Luxembourg, to work on farms in that Country for financial reasons. Farmers in Luxembourg owned larger parcels of land, were financially well off, and the Franc was of excellent value, while at that time the German currency was not worth anything. The border was only twenty kilometres away, although it was illegal for Germans to cross any border. I decided to give it a try, I wanted to make money and start planning for the future. It was 1948, and I was now sixteen. One of our neighbours sons, who worked in Luxembourg, made all the arrangements with a well to do farm family to hire me unseen, that is how desperate farmers were to get help. When I told my foster family that I was leaving, they took it very hard, but understood. My last evening there at dinner, the father started to cry, and sobbing, said, do not forget this is your home, this is where you belong, and I never did forget. As a matter of fact fifteen years later, when I got married, they stood in lieu of my parents, so did the family from Luxembourg, whom we have not met yet.

The next day I took the bus to the border town and waited for the dark. Arrangements had been made for the farmer's son to pick me up at a certain hour at the river, which was the border. It had rained for days and the river was swollen, the current was very strong and dangerous. At the arranged hour I saw a car across the river, flashing its lights, that was it. I stripped, stuffed my clothing into my suitcase and waded into the river, lifting the suitcase above my head. Pretty soon the water reached my chin, one slip, or wrong step, would have pulled me under. I told myself that I would let my suitcase go if I could not hold on, and swim to shore. But I made it. Across the river I met a young man in his early twenties, who ushered me into his car, I got dressed, and we proceeded to his parent's farm.

I was in for a surprise, the house and the yard turned out to be an old castle. The rooms were huge with high ceilings, wood fire places in every room. I was shown to a large room with patio doors leading out into the garden. The castle was situated on top of a hill, overlooking the town.

The family consisted of husband and wife, a son who had picked me up at the river, and was enrolled at the Luxembourg University, and a daughter, a very pretty girl in her mid twenties, who was at home waiting for her future husband. She certainly did not have a problem attracting young, eligible bachelors; however, none of the suitors was good enough for Madame, or should I say not rich enough. I do not want the reader to get the wrong impression, all married woman in Luxembourg have the title Madame, the French pronunciation. At this point I would like to mention that after the war Germans were very much disliked, even hated by some, as was the case in all previously occupied countries, and who can blame them, certainly not me. Luxembourg is a Grand Duchy, the people speak German, French and Luxembourgian, which is close to the Eifel dialect, I had learned across the border, so I had no problem understanding and conversing in their tongue.

The people I was with did not convey any animosity against Germans toward me, although they would have had reason to. The husband, a very compassionate man, well educated and generous to a fault, had been in a concentration camp, only because he had been the mayor in that town, and would not obey German orders. He was not very healthy and would never talk about his experiences in the camp. The wife had been the governess and educator in a 'French aristocratic family, she preferred to speak French, and took the time to teach me. The daughter was friendly, warm and outgoing. At community dances we danced a few times together, that raised a few eyebrows, in those days the girls did not fraternize with German young men, all that is changed now. The son was a little snobbish but friendly.

During the four years in Luxembourg I did all the things I had enjoyed doing in the little Eifel town. Played soccer, joined the church choir, and theatre groups, I also bowled. Sundays I sang the "Credo" solo during Mass and this was quite a feather in my cap. Mass was held in Latin of course. I became popular in many circles, and my new family was very proud of their German farmhand. All this meant, I had been accepted. Lesson learned, if you respect others, if you show compassion for your fellow men, and over all treat others as you would want to be treated yourself, nationalities matter not, you will gain respect, understanding and sometimes even friendship. All through my long life and career, I have been able to gain acceptance. Little did I know then that sixteen years later, in 1966 would I return from Canada, be married across the border, and be employed by the third largest chemical company in the world as Personnel Manager, in Luxembourg. Till that day, I had many more mountains to climb. In 1952 I returned to Germany, this time legally, across the bridge, spanning the river.

The economy in Germany had been growing rapidly. The West German government had implemented a new currency. In 1949 every German man, woman, and child was issued one hundred Marks; therefore, most people started on an equal footing. The German economic miracle was still a few years away. At least the black market was done with, food rationing was in the past, and there was an efficient new West German Federal Democratic Republic in place. The newest, and one of the most important allies of the U.S.A. Cities were being rebuilt, and some of the historic buildings were being restored to their old grandeur.

I stayed with my adoptive foster parents for a while, who were doing much better financially by now. They even owned a tractor and no longer did cows pull the plough.

There was an American Air Force base nearby, and I applied for a job as an air crash/rescue trainee, and was accepted. I lived with my foster parents and commuted to the base five days a week. Over the next six years I became quite familiar with military life, although civilian, I had many privileges the airmen enjoyed. Cheap purchases at the PX, cigarettes and alcohol, were a fraction of the costs we paid off base. Most important I could buy my foster mother all the coffee she wanted. She would give anything for a cup of real coffee, which had not been available in Germany since before the war. My English improved dramatically, and I became fluent in oral and written English. Professionally I moved into supervisory positions. At night I took university courses at the Trier University, and received my degree in business administration in 1957. Later on I had to do it all over again in Canada, even though I truly believe that education in German universities is superior to that in Canada.

During those six years on base, I participated in a lot of partying, I call it my wild years. Bars and strip joints became a way of life in many German towns and cities, located close to American and Canadian air force facilities. Quite often, after carousing and partying half the night, we returned to base, and I spent the night at the barracks with my new found buddies. There were plenty of vacant beds, as some of the personnel worked night shifts. This was also the time that I became sexually very active, not because I was driven to it, rather because it was expected of a healthy young man and everybody was doing it. Despite public opinion and knowledge, I became aware of a lot of homosexual activities happening in the military, even in those days when this was a taboo subject. When a man lives twenty four hours in close quarters with other men, who eat, drink, party, and shower together, some sexual encounters will take place. That does not necessarily mean that the participants are "Gay", for many it is just a pent-up sexual release, and part of being buddies. However soldiers were very careful not to be found out.

My view is that sex is much overrated, never in my life have I experienced the earth shaking passion that is supposed to be part of the sexual act, or the ringing of bells, and trembles when having an orgasm. To me it is not much different from masturbating. Maybe I am just different. I do however enjoy very much to cuddle and hug, and it is most pleasurable to feel the naked body of a person you care for, close to you when falling asleep in each others arms. All these things I can enjoy only with someone who wants me for the person I am, not for my looks, material things, or my position in life, someone that will try to get to know the real me. Most people that wanted to go to bed with me, and whom I slept with, did not possess those qualities. They are very superficial people, only interested in the pleasures of the moment. I find it hard to explain why, but in my whole life, which is slowly coming to an end, have I loved only once. That was forty years ago and ended in a deep hurt, I have never been able to love since, although I never gave up searching. To me the test of real love is that you always want to give and keep on giving, without expecting anything in return. Real love is when your eyes moisten by just looking at the subject of your love and affection and you feel like holding that person tightly, never wanting to let go—keep on dreaming.

In 1958 I decided to immigrate to Canada. If you ask me why, I do not have the answer. Germany was on its way to economic recovery, I was modestly successful, there were friends, even some people I considered family. Yet I was alone, and homeless, therefore I wanted to move, and keep on searching, what for I do not know. Canada was a country I knew very little about, and certainly there was no one over there I knew. Originally I wanted to move to the U.S.A. a country I knew from stories my Air Force buddies told me about during the past six years. However it was much more difficult to move to that country, for one thing you needed a sponsor over there. Over the next forty five years I found out that the urge to keep on moving, and the overwhelming restlessness would stay with me always. I was never content, satisfied or truly happy anywhere. The day my home was taken away from me, I lost my haven, my security, and my peace of mind. I truly believe that I always have been, and always will search for what was taken from me. For a few fleeting moments as a child at Oma and Opa's I did experience something very close to Utopia. Some people may call it a paradise lost. Later on in life I did make a lot of money and squandered it by subconsciously trying to rebuild what I had lost. It is not very realistic to be a dreamer.

Early in 1958 I went to Bonn, which was now the Capital of West Germany, and went to the Canadian Embassy to submit my immigration application. When I told my foster parents about my plans, they became very upset and tried very hard to dissuade me from going through with it. No use, when my mind is made up about something, I follow through with it. One of my other traits is, that I tend to make on the spot decisions, which can turn out to be good or bad. However, I have always been able to turn a negative into a positive, which is one of my strengths. In my lifetime, I have been completely down and out four times, to the point where the situation seemed to be hopeless, when most people would have given up, either killing themselves, or chosen a criminal path, a much easier life.

These desperate situations happened to me twice more later on while living in Canada, which I shall talk about in the second part of this book.

In May 1958 I received notification from the Canadian Embassy that I had been granted Landed Immigrant status. My ship was to leave Bremerhafen, (the port near the city of Bremen} on June 14 and my destination in Canada was Port Williams, Ontario, today Thunder Bay. A job as a fire/safety inspector was reserved for me at the Port Williams airport. This was all based on my training and experience with the American air force. As the reader will see, this plan would fly out the window due to another rash decision I made when I landed in Montreal, Quebec. Rather than having a secure job and a planned future in a new country, I ended up being a farm hand in Alberta. Everyone makes his own bed and has to sleep in it. The Department of Immigration paid my fare, which at that time came to Two Hundred Forty dollars, and had to be repaid as soon as I earned a wage in Canada.

My foster parents wanted to accompany me to Bremen to see me off. I asked them not to come, as I knew it would be too emotional for all of us. So we said our Goodbyes at the train station. We promised to write, which we faithfully did for the next nine years, that is when I saw them again, but more of that later. I left with one suitcase and fifty dollars in my pocket, the equivalent of Two Hundred German marks at that time. I stayed one night in Bremen, and the next morning boarded the "Seven Seas" in Bremerhafen.

The ships orchestra was playing "Auf Wiedersehn", and other old German tunes like "Muss I denn zum Staedtele hinaus" in later years made famous by Elvis under the title Wooden Heart, in the film G.I. Blues. There was a lot of hugging, kissing, and crying going on, and people waving from the ship to those staying behind. Paper streamers were flying through the air, and emotions running high. It was quite an experience.

I stood by myself, a stranger embarking into an unknown future, to an unknown foreign country. Homeless in my country of birth, and would be homeless in a new world. Over the years I would purchase and sell numerous houses and other properties, but none of them would be home. The day I leave this earth, I will be at peace.

PART II

1

The Voyage

When the "Seven Seas" left Bremerhafen in late June 1958, I felt no emotions whatsoever, I was just very alone. Leaving the country of my forefathers, a country that no longer was home to me, and literally sailing into the big unknown. I had one suitcase and about fifty dollars in my pocket, and owed the Canadian Government Two Hundred Forty dollars already without having set foot in Canada.

On board I shared a cabin with three other young Germans, and we quickly bonded.

We stopped in Le Havre France, and in Liverpool England, then it was eleven days on the ocean. With the exception of one day, the weather was beautiful. The meals were served in three settings, cabins were assigned certain times to eat in accordance with the cabin number. My new found buddies and I ate at the third setting. The one stormy day practically nobody went to the dinner table, we were all sick in our cabins. However, we made up for the one lost day and the food was always excellent. I remember getting to know a soft drink I had never tasted before called Ginger Ale, and I enjoyed it very much. My friends and I participated in many activities on board, card games, board games, Bingo, which was new to me, and we participated in all the dances at night. While I had been scheduled to go to Port Williams, Ontario, the other three were supposed to move on to Edmonton, Alberta once we landed in Canada. Although we studied the maps to find these locales, we really did not have a clue what those cities had to offer.

We arrived in Montreal June Twenty Seven, and went through Immigration, as one of the few people on board who spoke English, I was asked to translate for the Immigration Officers. I bargained with them to exchange my train ticket from Port Williams to Edmonton so that I could stay with my friends, and they obliged. Of course I never considered the fact that I gave up a decent job that was waiting for me in Port Williams. To me Canada was the land of plenty, with lots of opportunities, where anybody who tried could become rich quickly. Reality would hit me soon.

The four of us spent one day in Montreal, happy with our new found freedom. We felt like young colts, full of energy, ready to take on the world or at least Canada. The train ride from Montreal to Edmonton was uneventful, but I was amazed at the expanse of the country, the forests, lakes and wide open spaces in Manitoba and Saskatchewan, it reminded me a little of East Prussia. The other thing I noticed, were the tar paper shacks and generally depleted looking homes along the tracks, yards cluttered with junk. Most properties though had an impressive looking car sitting in the yard. To my eyes the farms and houses were a depressing sight, and I was not blinded by the pretentious looking big vehicles.

We arrived in Edmonton July 1, Canada Day, which meant every office and public building was closed. Two immigration officers met us at the train station, and took us to the old Alberta Hotel, located in the seedier section of the city. The four of us had to share one room and we were given meal tickets, which could be redeemed at a greasy spoon type restaurant across the street, called pretentiously The Blue Danube. What a dive, the place was frequented by prostitutes and pimps, quite a Welcome to a new country. There was also another noisy and wild hotel across the street called the Queens. Never in my life had I seen so many drunken fights at night on the sidewalk in front of these two hotels. Part of the night we heard the yelling, screaming and swearing and were unable to sleep. What really bothered me, were the numbers of intoxicated native people on the street. One time I saw two native women beat each other with the heel of their shoes, cursing and yelling at each other. In those days each pub had a separate entrance for males and males with escorts. I had never experienced that people went to pubs just to get drunk and fight. In Germany you went to a pub to enjoy yourself, have sing a-longs, and dance in the isles. There was always somebody playing the accordion, and everybody had a good time. In this new country they kicked you out if you dared to sing in a pub. This was strange to me, I thought no wonder there are so many alcoholics.

What was most upsetting to me though, were the number of down and out native people in front of these hotels, begging for money. My schoolbooks in Germany had shown the proud and brave Indians in North America who defended and fought for their identity and their culture. In school I had been impressed by their long rich history and their spirituality. Legends like Geronimo, Sitting Bull and Crazy Horse, were my childhood heroes. What I saw here made a mockery of everything I had learned, and made me feel very sad. It was twenty five years later, when I devoted my career to work with native people on their reservations, that I came to know the true spirit of native people and the rich traditional heritage they tried to preserve. I also learned to appreciate and participate in their ceremonies, most of all I believed in their teachings of love and sharing.

The day after the long weekend holiday we were supposed to visit the unemployment office in order to find out what jobs were available. We had no problem finding the office it was right downtown about five blocks from the hotel. In 1958 Edmonton had a population of about Two Hundred Thousand; the Mac Donald Hotel was the tallest building in town. When we arrived at the unemployment office they gave us an application to fill out, which I also did for my buddies, as they spoke no English and certainly could not communicate in writing. Then we were given the bad news that there were no jobs available, except as dish washers and farm hands, this was definitely a bad situation, one we had not anticipated. I felt for my friends who were unable to communicate in English. That evening in our hotel room, I told the others that I was willing to go and work on a farm, but that I was not prepared to add to my debt to the Government, we owed them already for the fare, the hotel and the meals, and this added up daily. Years later I learned that in North America it was a way of life to go into debt, which was encouraged to bolster the economy. One of my three friends also decided to join me in my venture. So the next day the two of us returned to the unemployment office and told the clerk of our decision. He provided us with two bus tickets to Camrose about sixty miles East of Edmonton, and told us to see the Town Secretary there. The next day we said Goodbye to the other two guys and boarded the bus. Although we promised to stay in touch, we lost track of each other. I started to regret already of not having gone to Port Williams, Ontario.

2

A New Start

The bus ride to Camrose was about one hour, it was Canada's newest city and very picturesque, it is called the rose city. The centre is located in a valley with a park and lake.

As it happened, the farmer's wives and children were having a picnic by the lake. When we arrived at city hall, the secretary told us he knew of several farmers who needed help most of them or their wives would be at the picnic, so he took us down there. He spotted a woman with three boys and talked to her. She called us over and introduced herself as Elaine. She told us, yes—they needed a farm-hand, and they also had a neighbour who was looking for help. When she realized that I spoke English, she opted for me. After a brief discussion we all went to her car, a station wagon, the biggest car I ever sat in. Her three boys, aged six to ten, were quite outgoing and asked a lot of questions. The farm was about four miles out of town. On the way there we stopped at a hog farm, where we dropped my friend off. The farmer seemed to be quite happy to get some help.

Elaine's husband's name was Art, and he seemed to be a bit surprised to see me when we got there. Over supper he told me that he actually had found help that day, but not to worry, I should stay the night and he would take me to other neighbours the next day who also needed help.

The farms in those days were of course not as modern and did not have the facilities as farms have today. Art's place had a few machine sheds, an old dilapidated barn, and the house, which was new and quite nice. It was a grain farm, two sections of land, and the only animals they had were two milk cows. Elaine was a teacher in Camrose, so together they had a decent income. The soil in that area was very good, and conducive to grain farming.

The next morning I got up early, and walked outside to look around, I thought everybody was still asleep, and was surprised to find Elaine in the old barn getting ready to milk the cows. I told her "Let me do it", and she seemed to be really happy that I could milk by hand. When I was done, and walked back to the house, Art announced that they had decided to keep me after all. Everybody, including the boys seemed to be happy. It was a wonderful family to be with, they made me part of it. I learned to run the tractor and harvesting machinery, but never got efficient with it. I realized that grain farming is not my cup of tea. My forte were animals; cattle, hogs, and horses. But irregardless, my time with this farm family was most enjoyable. Every Saturday we went into Camrose. Saturday nights we went to a drive-in theatre, which I had never seen before. Sundays I usually met my buddy at the hog farm, he was very unhappy. The farmer he was with was not very sociable. My friend had to eat by himself in the kitchen, and slept in a room attached to the garage. To make things worse, he was very homesick, although he earned a little more money than I did, I would not have traded with him.

I earned One Hundred dollars per month and did not spend one penny of it. Whenever we went to town, be it to a Drive-In Theatre or shopping, Art paid for everything. After about two month my friend was leaving the hog farm and returned to Germany, at least he had family back home to return to. I stayed with Art and Elaine through the summer and through completion of the harvest. In November I reluctantly told them that I would return to Edmonton, because I saw no future working on the farm. I was going to try for an office job in Edmonton and take university classes at night. Art wanted me to stay and suggested that he would like to diversify his operation; he felt that was the future of farming in Alberta. He was going to invest in beef cattle and hogs, we were going to build a farrowing barn and raise pigs until they were ready for market. The idea was that I was in charge of the cattle and hog operation, and we would be partners as far as the wiener production was concerned. I gave it a long thought, but decided against it, although I was very tempted, farming was in my blood. The three boys were growing up fast and I felt the future was uncertain if I remained there. The first of December I took the bus back to Edmonton. I stayed in touch with Art and Elaine and visited several times. As it turned out none of the boys stayed on the farm. The eldest is an engineer with an oil company in Saudi Arabia, the second one is a dentist and the youngest son is a senior manager with the department of agriculture. Art sold the farm and started a real estate firm in Camrose; he passed away about eight years ago.

In Edmonton I rented a room in a house close to downtown, it was owned by an elderly couple in their seventies, they had another renter across the hall from me; the room fully furnished was thirty dollars per month. Every day I pounded the pavement looking for work. The papers showed many ads for employment and I walked to every address no matter how far. I must have walked several hundred miles within a two week period. Anyway it seemed to be hopeless. Then one day I received a phone call regarding a job selling life insurance, it was one week to Christmas and I thought how nice it would be to have something to show for when the holidays came around. The caller asked me to meet him in a hotel at a certain time which I did. He was glib and a good talker and I was very naïve, definitely not worldly. He asked me how much money I had, that question should have rang alarm bells, but I was so desperate for a job, that I told him I had about two hundred dollars to my name. He persuaded me to invest that money into a life insurance policy; in return he would give me a job with his company. I could start my training the next day and I would work on a commission basis. The sky is the limit he said, what he did not say was how delighted he was to have met a sucker like me.

The next day I went to the office of the Insurance Company they handed me a number of forms and gave me a district to work in. I was supposed to go from house to house selling insurance, which was the training that had been offered to me. I looked completely out of place, dressed in an old winter jacked, old pants, worn out shoes, a toque and mitts. Can you imagine anyone buying insurance from such a character? I also was a very shy person who always found it difficult to approach total strangers, never mind selling them something.

Christmas came and I did not have one cent in my pocket. I had one loaf of bread in my room, and that was all I had for Christmas dinner. Christmas Eve I walked along Jasper Avenue cold, shivering and tears running down my face. Seeing all the decorations and happy faces, people carrying parcels shouting "Merry Christmas" to each other, all that activity made it worse. Not knowing a single person, lonely and hungry I went back to my room and cried myself to sleep. During this period in my life I developed a dislike for Edmonton, even though it is a beautiful city, to this day I associate Edmonton with loneliness, sadness and unfeeling, cold people. In contrast Calgary is the city I learned to love and the reader will soon see why. It may not be fair to Edmonton, but personally I believe that the dislike and the rivalry between the two cities go much deeper than economics and sports. To me Calgary has a soul and character, Edmonton has not. People in Calgary are mostly approachable, helpful and friendly, while Edmontonians seem to be the opposite.

In January 1959 I went to the Immigration Department, I was desperate and at the end of my wits, I practically begged them to help me find a job, and surprisingly they came through. A few days after my visit I received a phone call and I was asked to get ready we were going to Calgary for an interview. I do not believe that anyone in that department would walk that extra mile today to help a person in need. The next day the officer drove me to Calgary and a new episode in my life began, a much happier period that I still remember with fondness.

We arrived in Calgary on a cold but sunny winter day, and I was taken to an older, spacious house that was leased by the Government to be used as an interim shelter for destitute immigrants. There were several families in this house and I was shown to a room which became my own for the next two month until I was on my feet again. As I am writing this a smile comes to my face, because one of my favourite songs in later years became Michael Bolton's song "Back on my feet again."

The next day we went to the interview, which took place at the Lincoln Park Military Base in South West Calgary. The position I was interviewed for, was that of an Air/Crash Rescue and Safety Supervisor, I was told that based on my six years experience at the American Air Force Base in Germany, I would stand a good chance to get this job. Canadian Pacific Airlines operated an aircraft repair and test station at Lincoln Park; they employed a rescue and fire fighting crew of four men who were in need of a Supervisor and Instructor. The interview went well and the next day I was offered the position, and started work the same week. Part of the agreement was that Canadian Pacific would send me to Camp Borden, Ontario Air Force Base to attend a six weeks training program in air crash rescue, which took place the following month.

The four men I was to supervise and train, showed a lot of resentment toward me, and with some reason. I was not a Canadian; I was a D.P. (displaced person, not depressed prick). They had been working there from three to four years, and felt that one of them should have been promoted; also I was a few years younger than either one of them. One crew member in particular always tried to undermine my position, he was a Scotsman who always schemed behind the scene, never showing open hostility toward me, but I was aware of what he was up to. I believe in being up front with sub ordinates and superiors alike, manipulators are not my favourite people. Over the years I was able to prove myself, my life experiences and the teachings of my Opa had made me a natural leader and "People" person. For the rest of my life, have I been able to gain the respect and trust of people irregardless of who they were, or what situations they were in. I am quite proud of those strengths. The training in Camp Borden went well and I completed it successfully.

One day one of the test pilots offered to take me up into the air for a test flight, I was excited and happily accepted the offer. It was an old two seated Harvard fighter plane from the war and I was strapped into my seat behind the pilot. To this day I am not sure if what followed next was part of the testing process, or if the pilot was having fun with me. When we were air borne he started doing all kinds of stunts and manoeuvres, climbing straight up, nose diving, making loops, flying upside down to the point where I did not know which side was up. I was not scared just sick, sick, sick, I was not sure if I would be able to keep my food down, however, I managed until we landed, then everything spiralled and I let lose. Of course everybody thought it was hilarious.

My life was on an upswing, I rented my own room, purchased my first car, a 1949 Pontiac, that I paid Two Hundred dollars for, and started again to take university night classes, to have my degree from Germany validated. Despite my new found success I was alone and a loner, always searching to belong.

Early in 1960 I met a young man at a party who was in need of a room mate, his name was David, I moved in with him. David, his sister Rose, a nurse, and I shared a house together. I will always be grateful to him for making me part of a wonderful family, a family I adopted as my own, and who also adopted me. Today after forty three years they are still the only family I have. In particular Ena, whose full name is Nicklosina, and who is David's oldest sister, has become my dearest friend, confidant, and sister. Her three daughters are very close to me and their children are like my grand children. But I am getting ahead of myself, which is a bad trait to have. In the beginning Ena was not my favourite of David's siblings, she talked too much and was somewhat domineering. Maybe I am a male chauvinist, but I do dislike domineering women, possibly because I like being "In Charge", and am also very head strong, a typical German square head. As luck will have it, a few years later I ended up with a wife who was extremely dominant and almost drove me to commit murder.

David's mother lived in a small town in Southern Alberta, raising chickens and trucking them to Calgary where she sold them to her regular customers. She had a very hard life, immigrated as a young girl from Estonia to Canada, married young and had ten children, of which one died as an infant. The nine remaining children were Ena, Jack, David, Anne, Theresa, Rose, Mary, Peter and Cecilia. Her husband left when the children were small, Ena the eldest was Twelve, and helped raising her younger siblings. Mom, as I called her from the beginning, took me into her heart as her tenth child, she was more of a mother to me than my own mother ever had been. Mom and I were extremely close, and her death in 1993 was devastating to me. Why do we always lose those that we love the most?

The family was poor, and went through hard times, but because of that, each of the siblings became quite successful in their own way. They are close to each other, and I came to know what a real family life is all about, and enjoyed many memorable experiences with them, including family reunions every two years, which I attend.

Ena was first to move to British Columbia. She became a teacher and has been teaching for thirty years; however, my greatest admiration for Ena is her accomplishment of raising two very beautiful and successful daughters, and a third who was born a Down syndrome child. Francis is over forty years old now, she is very active, does attend school every day, is capable of doing housework, and handicraft. She also participates in special Olympic activities; particularly swimming, and all due to Ena's commitment. Francis and I are very close. Down syndrome children, that have the love of their family, are very loving themselves, and are incapable of hurting anyone. I am always aware of how sensitive this forty year old child is.

In the sixties the rest of the siblings lived in Alberta. Anne, a very serious and religious woman, and her family were actually our neighbours. Dave, Rose, and I lived in the same house. Mom always wanted me to marry Rose, we used to go out dancing and dining, but marriage in those days was far from my mind. I really started to enjoy parties, and we had many in our house. I really involved myself in my new-found family life. Mary, her husband, and I went bowling together. They also enjoyed playing poker, and quite often we played all night long.

One day in 1964, we had a big birthday party for David. The whole family was there, including Ena, who had come from B.C. Anne and I did the cooking. Afterwards we danced and also consumed some alcohol. Jack and his wife Doris became quite amorous, which was fine; however, they were still very young, and had four children already. They had been school sweethearts, and married while still in their teens. On the other hand, they were also very naïve, did not have a clue about birth control, but now at the party they wanted to go and have sex. I took Jack upstairs, and gave him a condom, and showed him how to use it and they went to their car to enjoy themselves. Later that night I woke up from a big commotion Doris was crying "I know I am going to be pregnant again". Rose, who was a nurse, trying to console offered her a douche. Anyway, from what I could put together, the condom either broke, or Jack put it on wrong, but Doris became pregnant again. Lucky for me, because their fifth baby, a boy, became my Godson.

David's Dad also lived in Calgary. He was an alcoholic, and lived with a lady who shared his love for alcohol. We visited them regularly, although there was no closeness. I found him to be a very nice person. He died quite young.

Canadian Pacific closed their operation in 1963 and moved to Vancouver, B.C. I had the choice of remaining with them or staying in Calgary without a job. I decided to stay in Calgary.

I loved the city and the people. My adopted family was there and I became quite the fanatic sports fan. Hockey and football were new to me, but I became an enthusiastic follower of both. In those days it was the old Calgary Stampeder hockey team in the Western League, whose biggest rivals of course were the Edmonton Flyers. To this day I am a Calgary Stampeder football and Calgary Flames hockey fan. Of course with the recent losing run of the Flames, I take a lot of ribbing from people in these parts of Alberta, where the majority of the people are Edmonton sports fans.

After Lincoln Park closed I found several jobs in the hotel business, from dishwasher, busboy, waiter, to bartender. In my whole life I was never too proud to tackle even the most demeaning jobs, and I was always successful in whatever I did. What I could not handle was abuse by customers who thought that due to their station in life, or due to their inherited wealth, could look down on the people that had to serve them. Case in point—I was a waiter at the prestigious Calgary Golf and Country Club. Peter Lougheed at that time was a successful lawyer, and was a member of the club. I found him to be a very considerate and down-to-earth person. His wife was a different story. One night shortly before closing, Mrs. Lougheed arrived with four other ladies, and I was given their table. They were most unpleasant and very demanding. First, there was something wrong with the drinks, and then the menu was not to their liking. So it went, they ordered me back and forth, demanding this and that. In the meantime, I became more and more agitated. Finally, when I served them the soup Mrs. Lougheed complained it was too cold, and chased me back to the kitchen. By that time I was so upset that I dumped the fresh hot soup in her lap, an accident, of course. A big commotion ensued and the Maitre D' was called, but before he could open his mouth, I told him that I quit, and walked out. Little did Mrs. Lougheed know then, that eight years later I would be a senior manager in her husband's government. I, of course, did not know that either.

On Canada Day 1963 I became a Canadian citizen. The brief ceremony took place at the Calgary courthouse, and I swore allegiance to the Queen; therefore, I became a British subject. At that time I was not in full agreement with this, I wanted to be a Canadian, not a subject of royalty. Finally, when Pierre Elliott Trudeau repatriated the constitution this became true. To this day I am Canadian first and an Albertan second. As controversial as Mr. Trudeau may have been, particularly in the west, I truly believe he was the best Prime Minister this country has ever had. He had vision, he was an intellectual, yet bold and colour-ful, above all, he had a backbone. He would have stood up to President Bush's politics of aggression today, and not have succumbed to the President's blackmail tactics to disfavour those countries that don't fall in line.

I was fed-up with my life, having to serve on people, and having to jump every time they snapped their fingers. I was intelligent, had an IQ of over 140, was well educated, and eager to see what other things I could experience. So in February 1964 I applied for the position of a fire/safety supervisor position in Fort Churchill, Manitoba. This was a rocket Research centre, a co-operation between the Canadian Research Council (CRC) and NASA. The base was operated by Pan AM Airlines, and I became an employee of Pan Am.

3

Churchill, Manitoba

The town of Churchill is located on the shores of the Hudson Bay in the most northern part of Manitoba. Churchill is also a harbour that is open for three months during the summer. Those three months were a boom for Churchill. Large cargo ships from all over the world entered the harbour daily, to be loaded with wheat from the prairies. The two hotels were jumping and doing very well due to all the sailors that stayed over for two to three days partying and drinking. It was not uncommon for these young men to get drunk, pick up a case of beer and an equally drunk native woman, and leave together. No wonder that cases of gonorrhoea and syphilis in Churchill were skyrocketing.

I arrived in Churchill by plane from Winnipeg on a cold, blistery day; it was about—40 degrees Celsius. Later I found out that sometimes temperatures dropped to—60 degrees below and colder with the wind chill. There were days when we were forbidden to go outside, because any exposed human flesh would have frozen within thirty seconds. Living quarters and public facilities were connected by covered walkways or tunnels. So that the reader will not get confused, I must explain that there is the town of Churchill, and the base of Fort Churchill, connected by highway of approximately ten miles. Half way between Churchill and Fort Churchill, was a navy base. Another ten miles from Fort Churchill was the rocket research centre. There was a shuttle bus service between Fort Churchill, the navy base, and Churchill town every half hour. Anyway, I lived in Fort Churchill in a barracks type setting. There were approximately two thousand men, comprised of air force, civilian, and NASA personnel. There were only about one hundred women (nurses and secretaries), in most cases available to officers and senior management only.

Fort Churchill had all amenities, from cinemas to bowling lanes, as well as banks and clothing stores. However, meals were taken in the mess halls. If you wanted to drink or eat in a restaurant, you took the shuttle to town. There was no fee to use the bus.

I later became a member of the officers club at the navy base; one of the officers who also had his family there sponsored me. We became very good friends. Drinks at the navy base were twenty five cents, the navy put on many dances and parties, which I usually attended.

The rocket site was of course a restricted area, and we were picked up by bus for our shifts, or when the firing of rockets was scheduled. That was dependent on the Boreal Aureoles (northern lights). The research had to do with the effect northern lights had on plants, animals, and humans. How the lights were created? Could they be useful for certain things, etc? My job required the fire/safety inspections in all buildings on base, and the rocket site; besides lectures to all personnel, fire training of the rocket crews and standby during every launch. The job was interesting, the money was good, with a special northern allowance, and the benefits were even better. Six weeks paid vacation every year, and as a Pan Am employee, I paid only ten percent airfare to any location in the world that Pan Am flew to. During my three year stint in Fort Churchill, I visited Central and South America, Europe, Japan, and Hong Kong. It was during those travels that I really broadened my horizon and outlook on life. Every country I visited I rented a car and travelled the small towns and villages, avoiding tourist centres. I rather visited and associated with the poor and under-privileged population in some of these countries. And believe me, there are a lot more people in this world poor, hungry, sick, and generally down trodden, than those well-to-do, particularly in some of the South American countries. Hong Kong, a city pulsating with energy, business and wealthy people, also had the millions of Chinese refugees living and starving in tents in the hills surrounding the city. It sure opened my eyes.

Returning from one such trip I decided to take the train from Winnipeg to Churchill, we called it the Tundra Express. It was a three day trip, but worth it. Through the Northern parts of the Province the train crawled along, a man could have run next to it and keep up. We could feel the train swaying, the ground underneath was pure muskeg. I enjoyed that trip, the scenery was beautiful and there was always a party happening, you met some very interesting and colourful people on board. To get to Churchill you either had to take the Tundra Express or fly in, the highway ended in The Pas, Manitoba.

The three month of summer in the North were very beautiful. The Tundra was a multi coloured carpet of blossoms, there was almost twenty four hours of daylight, however, I found it difficult to sleep at night. During these three months all plant life grew rapidly, we had plenty of blueberries, but the giant horse flies and mosquitoes made it an adventure to stay in one place too long.

Churchill had also a mix of Inuit and Native Canadian population; I noticed a big difference in the life style of these two cultures. The Inuit made a living of whaling and fishing, and worked in the whaling plant others held permanent jobs on base. When I visited their homes, they made you feel welcome and offered some food. Their houses were kept immaculate and they did not drink alcohol. On the other hand the native people lived of Government handouts, their homes were tarpaper shacks, and substance abuse was rampant.

In the spring polar bears were a common sight, they were beautiful animals, quite brazen when they wanted food, but also very dangerous and unpredictable, in particular females with their cubs. They floated in to shore when the ice broke, and walked right into your kitchen if they knew the place and had been given food before. On occasion they would break the door down if they could smell food. Although it was forbidden to feed the bears, we did it all the time. I have seen the bears enter the large kitchen at the rocket launch site grab a plate with food and while holding it between their giant paws, eat all the food and even lick the plate, never breaking it. On one occasion this foolish practice cost NASA millions of dollars. We were getting ready for launch, everything seemed to be going according to plan, then at about minus twenty and counting we lost communication with the radar and telemetry crew. I took my truck to the radar site, about five miles away in order to investigate the problem. When I arrived, I found the two radar personnel in the attic, while a polar bear was destroying all the equipment in search of food. As the window for launch is often very small, the program had to be scrapped for that night and the next few days following, as the weather conditions were unfavourable to try another launch with success.

In June 1966 I decided to take another vacation, this time my plan was to fly to Germany, visit all my friends in Germany and Luxembourg. I booked passage from Winnipeg to New York with a one week stop over in the "Big Apple", and on from New York to Frankfurt. While in New York I took in the nightlife to the fullest; Broadway, Forty Second Street, Greenwich Village and Times Square, and also the Bowery and other not so popular districts. I have always been very adventurous and often on my travels I have ventured into areas that others would consider dangerous, I wanted to see and meet people that were disadvantaged not always through their fault.

The night before leaving for Germany, I was mugged on the street late at night, Three men attacked me and knocked me down, taking my wallet with two thousand dollars in traveller cheques in it, they disappeared before I could collect myself, of course it was foolish of me to carry that much money with me. I reported the incident to the police right away and the next morning I took a cab to the American Express office. What a surprise all their commercials advertising replacement of lost or stolen cheques within twenty four hours, was just B.S. They used all kind of excuses, and delayed my flight for another day. The next day they advised me to go on my trip and they would forward the money to me via Western Union within a week. I had to leave as I had no money; luckily I had my plane ticket.

A lot of changes had taken place in Germany since my departure eight years before. Prosperity was noticeable everywhere, cities had been rebuilt; old historic buildings had been restored to their old beauty. However, it was too dangerous for me to go to East Germany, and to go to East Prussia and my place of birth was out of the question. Since I had been born there, the Soviets would have considered me a Russian citizen, and possibly exiled me to Siberia, even though I was a Canadian now. I stayed with my previous foster parents who lent me some money to hold me over. The weeks of my vacation were spent travelling, visiting, partying, dancing and not always in that order. I spent a lot of time on the American Air force base I had worked on eight years before, made new friends and together we frequented every bar and strip joint in abundance near military bases. As usual I was the big spender; soldiers did not have much money. You always have a lot of friends when you have money. I always thought I was making up for lost time during my teen years, today I know that all through my life have I tried to buy friendship and love to overcome my loneliness. That was the case then and has haunted me through the years, I always was and always will be a "Giver" not a "Taker", that's why I am so easily taken advantage of.

I also visited the girl that I had been very fond of many years before; she, her youngest brother, and her mother lived by themselves now in a large new mansion. Her other siblings, two brothers and sisters had all moved away, married and were well established. I spent a lot of time at Kathrine's house; her mother treated me like one of her children. She was a wonderful, warm and loving woman, who had lost her husband in the war, and had raised her children to become decent and respectable adults.

After approximately three weeks I finally received a letter from American Express, it included one of my stolen Traveller Cheques with a forged signature on it. They asked me to verify that it was not my signature, which was obvious it did not come close. Finally, one week before I was due back in Churchill, I received all my money. I repaid my foster parents and still had a bit left over. At that time the exchange rate was one American dollar to four German marks, but the buying power was one to one. Kathrine and I started to talk marriage, I thought it was a good idea, I yearned to have my own family, and it certainly was time. I was thirty two and had become a true bachelor, I did not look forward to being tied down, yet wanted to be part of a stable family, and have children of my own to carry on my family name. Today I realize that these are all the wrong reasons to get married, however, Kathrine's reasons were not much better, she worried of becoming a spinster, who would be left alone with her brother who was a Manic Depressive, and having to care for her mother who was getting on in years. Kathrine was thirty at the time. We agreed that I would return to Churchill, resign from my job, and we would marry in September. We would remain in Germany as long as Kathrine's mom was alive and then she would come with me to Canada. By marrying me she would become a Canadian citizen. As we shall see later, the best plans don't always work out.

Before I left, I visited an American factory which was about to go into production across the border in Luxembourg, which was a twenty mile drive from my future home. They were advertising for some Bilingual supervisory personnel, as all their policies and procedures were written in English, all of their two thousand workers were German speaking; however, all managers were American and in most cases did not speak German. This was a Synthetic Fibre plant owned by the third largest chemical company in the world, which employed more than ninety thousand employees, and operated fifty eight factories world wide, producing anything from synthetic fibre to fertilizers and weed killers. I was well received by the Personnel Manager and the Plant Director, and I explained my situation to them. The interview was of course conducted in English and I could tell that they were very much interested in my services. We agreed that I would see them again upon my return from Canada in late August.

I returned to Churchill, gave my mandatory one month notice and packed all my belongings, I had quite a collection of Inuit soapstone carvings and native artefacts, in rocket crates, and shipped it all by freighter to Germany. Before I left Churchill, I invited my Manager and his family to come to my wedding. He had a son stationed in Germany and planned to visit him at the same time.

I left Churchill in late August; the wedding was set for September 17, 1966. Churchill and the North had grown on me, when I had arrived two years earlier, I never expected to leave with sadness in my heart, but I did. Everything happened so rapidly, I had no time to think. My adoptive family in Canada would not be able to afford a trip to Germany in those days. It had been arranged that I would stay with my foster parents to the day of the wedding, in the very staunch Catholic part of Germany, it would not have been proper to stay in the bride's house. Upon my arrival in Germany, I visited the Personnel Manager at the Nylon factory in Luxembourg and was offered the position of Supervisor,

Recruitment and Training, to start October 1, two weeks after my wedding. My salary would be the highest I had ever received in my career, as I realized much later, I was making more money than anybody in the town my wife and I lived in, and she made sure that everybody knew about it. My career growth potential with the company was unlimited. All I had to do now was to sit back and await my fate as a married man.

4

A Most Successful Career and a Disastrous Marriage

Our wedding day was a big event in my wife's hometown. It was a beautiful sunny September day and the church was packed for the ceremony. I was told afterwards that my face was very pale, and that while kneeling at the altar, people in the front rows could see the price tag on the soles of my new shoes. We had about three hundred invited guests, my wife came from a large family, and I only had my foster parents and their sons, my previous employer from Luxembourg and my Manager and his family from Canada. We had a Gourmet Luncheon and cocktails at the mansion, and then as was the custom, the whole wedding party went for a stroll through the town, while the bride and groom accepted congratulations and best wishes from the towns people, we handed out drinks, and invited everyone to the reception, dinner and dance in the evening, which took place in a large tent next to the pub.

It was a very successful evening. The wedding night however, did not fulfil my expectations. We had taken a suite in a hotel in Trier, and were leaving the next day on our honey moon in Italy. While Katherine was quite passionate, I performed as was expected from me, but with a very detached mind. It was as if my body was functioning but my heart was not in it, and I am certain that Katherine felt that something was amiss. I knew then that this marriage was wrong and that it had happened for all the wrong reasons, but I promised myself to be a good husband and father if we ever had a family. Because sex did not seem that important to me, I thought there might be something wrong and I felt sexually inadequate, secretly I wished that I was this Macho stud who was capable of satisfying the most demanding woman. As we both wanted children, we kept on trying.

I was very successful in my job, four promotions within five years and with my income we became quite accustomed to a lavish and privileged life style. I purchased a new luxury car each year, I bought my wife very expensive jewellery, and the most fashionable clothes, complete with matching hats, hand bags and shoes, all without her being present. The sales ladies were amazed at my taste in fashions and told me what a lucky woman my wife must be. Katherine was always the talk of the town, when she showed off her new attire Sunday's in church, and I of course was proud like a peacock. Today I realize of course that I wanted her to be as elegant as my own mother had been. We also completely remodelled the mansion and bought all new furnishings, predominantly oak and leather.

In 1967 my Company accepted the Management by Objectives philosophy. I took the Trainer of Trainers course for this program and travelled all fifty eight factories world wide to train their Managers in the new Management Philosophy based on Peter Drucker's Theory. This process took about two years, and kept me away from home most of the time, which caused more marital problems. On one hand Katherine became more demanding all the time and wanted more and more, she kept on pushing me to be even more successful, on the other hand she complained that I was never home, her favourite expression was "Are You married to that Company or me", this of course drove me nuts. We purchased a villa on the Costa Brava in Spain, where we spent our vacations. Katherine had two miscarriages over a period of three years, and her Gynaecologist advised her that the next pregnancy could be dangerous. That was a blow to both of us, but more so to her, I suggested adoption, but she strongly objected, some old fashioned upbringing made her believe that an adopted child could have inherited some bad traits from their biological parents. For example if one of the parents had a criminal background or lived of the avails of prostitution, the child could have inherited such behaviour. I was unable to talk her out of it.

My friend David from Calgary kept corresponding with me, this way I was always aware what was happening to my adopted siblings and mom. He had sold the house in Calgary and was homesteading in the Evansburg area in Alberta. Most of his brothers and sisters had gradually moved to British Columbia with their families. Our mom had a common law husband and had moved to Northern Alberta. I also kept in contact with Jack and Doris and sent presents to my godson. I asked Dave to suggest to Jack and Doris to let me adopt my godson John. They would not hear of it although they were struggling in those days and had five small children. I did not expect them to give John up; it was wishful thinking on my part.

Three years into my marriage another loss, Katherine's mother died of cancer. She, in her quiet and unassuming manner, had been the glue that kept the family together since she lived with us, all of Katherine's brothers and sisters with their families visited often, and spent weekends and holidays with us.

The funeral was very big, my Mother-in-Law was much respected and admired in our town, and her family had resided there for generations. My employer made certain that all senior managers and directors attended the funeral, which gave Katherine more status in town. After the burial the brothers and sisters all got together to discuss dispersal of all the properties their mother had left behind. In her will everything was supposed to be divided evenly including our mansion and the land surrounding it, this was not feasible and created problems. I of course was excluded from the discussions as were all the In Laws, all I had to do is pay dearly in the end. Apparently it was quite a session and arguments heated up, it never fails to amaze me how a close knit family starts feuding when a loved member of the family passes on. I saw the same thing happening when my mom in Canada died many years later, although mom did not have many possessions. She had left me some items which I never received however; I am not the type of person who will make a big fuss.

Anyway Katherine had agreed with her brothers and sisters to divide our property three ways, her younger brother not included as she agreed that we would always look after him, and I would pay all three a certain amount of money, which was quite a large amount, she agreed to all this without consulting me first. I happened to be the cash cow, or bull as may be. My plan had always been to return to Canada after mother's death, and she had agreed to that. Now she did not want to hear of it and it damaged our relationship further with no mother around to calm the waters.

In 1969 my company opened a new factory in the Northern part of Germany. I was seconded there to do all the preliminary work, recruit all management personnel, develop policies and procedures, negotiate tax and other benefits with the Provincial Government of Westphalia, have discussions with the Unions and try to keep the plant non union, which in Germany was rather difficult, I rented an apartment in that town and drove home on weekends only.

The workload, responsibilities and the constant confrontations and unhappiness at home, took its toll, our life style, plus having to pay Katherine's brothers and sisters, caused more frictions, there was never enough money, no matter how many salary increments I had. I went home less frequently and started visiting well known night spots in places like Hamburg and Cologne. After two Years of this mental abuse I was exhausted and near a mental break down, my physician gave me two years to live. It came to the point where in my darkest hours I considered killing Katherine. In 1971, during our last vacation together at the Costa Brava, I seriously considered letting our boat capsize and swim back to shore, Katherine was terrified of water and could not swim. When the monstrosity of this thought dawned on me, I decided divorce and return to Canada was the only way out. An ugly, lengthy divorce would have finished me, so I agreed to leave Katherine everything, I packed one suitcase, bought an airline ticket to Edmonton, Alberta, kept Five Hundred dollars and left. My ex wife wrote to me several times to plead with me to return, but I refused. People should never get married for the wrong reasons. So I was down again, but not out.

5

Canada, My Second Chance

Not much had changed in Edmonton in the eight years I had been away, two years in Churchill, and six in Germany. Although the skyline was changing, more high-rise buildings and the population had grown to over four hundred thousand. There were no more separate pubs for ladies and escorts, native people had the right to go anywhere they wanted no longer restricted to their reservations, although their plight became more visible all the time, and started to attract the attention of the International Community. The native population grew at a rate much faster than that of other origin in Canada, seven percent compared to less than two percent in the rest of the Country. With limited or no education, no economic development and no infra structure, they depended even more on Government handouts. A few reserves were fortunate to have oil discovered on their land and started to have a more prosperous existence.

However in the fall of 1971 I did not think very much about Native Canadian problems, personally I was a mess, having barely escaped a nervous breakdown, being severely overweight, lack of self esteem and a very heavy smoker, I was in dire need to recover and rescue what was left of my life. As it turned out David's homestead was the cure no doctor could prescribe. I took the bus to Evansburg, David's mailing address and went to the post office to ask the postmaster the location of the homestead. He had a vague idea and told me it was about eight miles from town in the middle of nowhere, a dirt road of four miles off the gravel road leading to the place. The road was passable only in dry summer conditions, and completely snowed in during the winter. This was August so the road was dry and the postmaster offered to take me there for ten bucks.

When I saw the place, I felt like turning back. It looked deserted, there was some cleared land, in the middle of it a small two room cabin, some sheds and corrals put together with slabs. A young girl about fifteen stood in the yard and greeted me, "Uncle Ernie" she called out. I did not know who she was, as it turned out it was Rose's eldest daughter, she had been only eight years old when I had seen her last. Rose and her new husband had a lot of problems with her, and David had agreed to look after his niece and offered her a lot of "Tough Love" in order to straighten her out, fat chance. David was quite happy to see me, not only to have company but also to help him with his operation. He had been given two quarter sections of Crown Land by the Government and had agreed to clear a certain number of acres per year over a five year period, before he would receive title to the property. There was no running water, he had dug a well by hand about two hundred yards from the cabin, no power no phone no natural gas. The cabin was heated by a wood stove, it was also used for cooking, and wood of course was in abundance. This man was able to live on about five hundred dollars per year. He had some chickens, sheep and goats, these provided meat, milk and eggs, vegetables he grew himself, and the only items purchased in a store, were flour, tea, sugar and margarine. He had also built a greenhouse to grow tomato plants and vegetables in early spring, then planted out in the cleared land, harvested and sold in the farmer's market in Evansburg.

This is the environment I stumbled into, a lean mean cuisine, with back breaking work and sweat and tears. Sometimes we did not see a single person for months on end. In the evenings we played cards by the light of a kerosene lamp, and we fought a lot, both of us took the games seriously and wanted to win. Slowly I became healthy again in body and mind, within three month I lost about sixty pounds and had developed a muscular body. I still had my five hundred dollars and I was determined to buy a milk cow, I did not care for goat's milk, I also wanted to make butter and cheese. One day in November we took the old truck, and left for the Drayton Valley auction. I bought a very nice looking Holstein heifer which was due to calf in December and I paid two hundred dollars for her. She was wild beyond belief, I sat in the back of the truck, in bitter cold weather, holding on to the rope with all my strength, as the cattle rack was very rickety and could not be trusted to hold the wild animal.

We were also constructing a large root cellar, the walls made of solid tree trunks, which we carried on our backs to the cellar. In December my heifer had a calf and by now she had become a pet and followed me around wherever I went. This meant we had fresh milk and I could make butter. I learned to bake bread, cheesecake and made the best cinnamon buns in the country. I no longer missed the life I left behind at all. The life of the rich, career, and parties were no longer important, I was quite content.

David was very frugal, held on to the money he had left from the sale of his house in Calgary, and was not prepared to expand the farming operation. I wanted to take out a loan to start a cow/calf operation and go into a partnership with him. However, he was not interested.

In February my cow needed to be bred again, we were of course snowed in, so I led her by a halter and rope, walking four miles through snow drifts and bitter cold to the nearest neighbour who had a bull. After we were done and my young cows desires were stilled, we started on our way back and had to walk against the wind, the cow was very stubborn, but we finally made it, although my cheeks and ears were frozen. This was also the time to start the greenhouse going. We planted about one thousand tomato seeds in single pots, as well as other vegetable seeds. We always took turns to sleep in the greenhouse as the stove had to be stoked at all times.

In April Rose, her new husband and their two small children, Grant 4, and Scott 2, arrived, they had decided to move to Australia, and wanted to make a trip across Canada in their motor home, Christina Rose's daughter from her first marriage and David were to go with them on this tour. They were gone for about five weeks and during that time I never saw a single person, I was happy in my solitude. Spring arrived early and May was very warm, to the point that I could skinny dip in the beaver dam, the beavers were so tame, and they swam with me. I became quite anxious to get things done out in the field and started to plant all the tomatoes. Late in May we had a severe night frost, and one thousand tomatoes plants were history. A few days later David returned from his trip. Rose was to spend one more weekend with us before going to Vancouver to depart for Australia. Mom came to visit and see her favourite daughter off.

David was irate and in my opinion actually unreasonable about the whole tomato affair, when you are farming or in his case pretend to, you must be aware that weather conditions can be the farmer's best friend or worst enemy. Unfortunately science has not been able yet to influence the weather. There was a lot of shouting and we almost came to blows, he blamed me for the whole fiasco. I packed my suitcase and walked the four miles to our neighbour who owed me some money for having helped him during the previous year's harvest. Mom tried her best to hold me back, she even sent Rose's husband after me, to no avail, when this square head's mind is made up, a team of horses would not change my direction.

I did not see Rose again for thirty years at the family reunion at Jack's and Doris's in 2001. David's homestead has become a very scenic place with a large new house, running water, power and all modern amenities. I took the bus to Edmonton and started anew again at age thirty eight.

Edmonton was experiencing a construction boom, Mill Woods, Sherwood Park and St. Albert were expending rapidly and I had no problem finding work immediately as a construction labourer, digging ditches and laying water and sewer pipes. It was hard work but healthy and the pay was good. All this time I kept on applying for positions in the Personnel Management field with Private Industry and the Government, I was well qualified with my degree in Business Administration and my five years with the chemical company in Luxembourg and Germany. Finally in the spring of 1972, I was interviewed and offered a position by the Provincial Government with the Department of Social Services and Community Health, as Supervisor Recruitment and Selection. It was the largest Department within the Government with more than eleven thousand employees, consisting of Social Workers, Psychiatrists, Youth Workers and Counsellors, working out of various offices across the Province. I had a staff of six recruiters, and we travelled a lot interviewing candidates in all parts of the Province. For senior management and senior professional positions we interviewed across the country from Vancouver to Montreal. I enjoyed this work tremendously, and my success rate in recruiting professionals with potential was rather high. I believe that my experiences in life had made me a good judge of character, and also of people's honesty and dependability.

Two years into my tenure, the Deputy Minister, the Director of Social Services and I departed on a recruitment trip to Winnipeg and Toronto. We were in need of two Senior Managers to take over the South and West Edmonton District Offices. South Edmonton served the population south of the North Saskatchewan River, Sherwood Park and the County of Strathcona. The West Edmonton Office included the area West of 109 Street, St. Albert and Parkland County. Each office employed a staff of one hundred to one hundred and thirty professionals respectively. On this particular trip we were successful in recruiting one candidate, but were unable to find a suitable second one. I told the Deputy Minister that I would like the chance to take a run at one of those positions. It had been the practice of the Department to promote or recruit people into these Senior Management positions who possessed a degree in Social Work and had worked many years in the field. I was able to convince the Deputy that the large offices would be operated more efficiently by people with administrative experience, able to manage a large budget and above all someone who had people management skills, therefore I was their man. I also had familiarized myself with all the pertinent policies, as well as the Child Welfare Act, I also stated that I was the right person to supervise and direct a staff of professionals, due to my strength in communicating and developing positive attitudes in people. To my delight I was given the position on a six month trial basis, which developed into eight years of success. These events created quite a stir in the Department, all my future colleagues shook their collective heads and forecasted gloom and doom; it was unheard of that someone with no social work or child welfare experience took over the largest office in the Province. Well I proved everybody wrong, my office became known as fiscally responsible, and most important had the lowest staff turnover rate and the fewest client complaints to the Minister's office.

The West Edmonton office specialized in child welfare apart from the regular Social Assistance programs. We were responsible for the well being of more than Three Thousand children in care, some Nine Hundred foster homes, and all adoptions in the Edmonton area. The Enoch First Nation was also within my jurisdiction, and I learned more about native people and their escalating problems.

For the first three years in my new position I lived in the luxurious penthouse in one of the new high rises overlooking the North Saskatchewan River valley. My income was quite high and I could afford luxuries that I had been unable to attain since my work in Germany. Seeing the plight and hardships of some physically and mentally abused children, and the lack of foster homes, particularly for older children, I decided to foster myself, without remuneration of course. I also did a lot of volunteer work and contributed financially to numerous child care causes. In 1977 I became a member of the Edmonton Child Abuse Committee, comprised of judges, paediatricians, psychiatrists and educators. This committee reviewed, discussed child welfare issues and made recommendations to the Minister's office, me being the liaison. During my years with the Government I raised four children, age nine to eighteen. All except one finished school, participated in sports, one attended university, and became a dentist. I drove them to school every morning before going to work, later when a bought my first acreage, they would have to take the school bus. I was tired of city life, deep inside I was always a country boy, and yearned for the personal freedom the country provided. So in 1977 I bought an acreage within commuting distance to Edmonton, and I never left the country again, for me the city was there to visit, not to live in. The children had their own horses, we had a milk cow and all kinds of fowl and other creatures, and I did a lot of gardening and landscaping, which gives me a lot of pleasure and peace of mind. In the winter I took the children to Disneyland, Mexico and for visits with my own adopted family. Today they are married, two still regard me as their dad, and I am a grandfather to their children. One son became heavily involved with drugs and alcohol and I still support him as much as I can. Every summer Ena and her daughter Frances visited me and do so to this day. Quite often I visit her and the family in B.C. Mom was still in North East Alberta, but also visited the acreage at least once a year.

In 1981 I became restless again, I wanted to do more, and I wanted to be involved in ventures that were not dictated by policies, procedures and red tape. I am a firm believer that when you leave for work, you must do so with a happy frame of mind, if going to work becomes a chore, you should quit, you also must return from work with a sense of accomplishment. All this was no longer happening, some of my colleagues at the ripe age of forty plus, had settled in to a comfortable rut, twiddling their days away and waiting for a lucrative retirement. I did not want this happening to me, they thought I was nuts when I announced my resignation, giving up the security of a well paying job and a Senior Manager's pension that would have amounted to four thousand dollars per month by the time I retired, which would have been in 1999. Before I resigned of course I had secured another position, that of an Operations Manager with the Enoch First Nation, I had agreed to a one year legal contract, renewable from year to year. For the next eighteen years I dedicated all my efforts to improve life on Indian Reservations, and never strayed from that goal no matter what obstacles I would encounter. In later years I found that it was an easier task to work with the so called "Have not" First Nations, than it was with the wealthier ones. Enoch, my first venture was a wealthy reserve at that time with an abundance of producing oil wells.

The Department gave me a big send off, they rented a large banquet room in a large hotel and some four hundred people attended the banquet and dance, there were speeches and gifts, but also some tears, mostly from my own staff. Thus ten years of my career with the Government came to an end. However, in years to come I found that the relationships I had fostered, and my knowledge of Government procedures were quite helpful in my work with native people.

6

Politics & Canada's First Nations

During my eighteen years of direct involvement with the native people in Alberta, I have gained a lot of understanding of their hardships and their constant struggle to be accepted by the dominant Caucasian society in Canada. They want and need equal opportunities in life. It has been a slow and hard process, but I believe that native people have come further and have made greater strides toward self determination, self reliance, and in particular awareness of their own worth, their pride, and their power, over the past twenty years, than the two centuries prior. Most of this progress has been due to education and with it the realization that progress does not mean losing your culture, your spiritual ways, and your own language.

Our forefathers were more than short-sighted when they signed the treaties about two hundred years ago in the east, and one hundred twenty years ago in the west.

Across Canada there are more than five hundred reserves with a population of about six hundred thousand. Alberta has forty three reservations—Treaty Seven in the south, consisting of six First Nations. Treaty Six which stretches from B.C. through central Alberta and into Saskatchewan has seventeen First Nations, and Treaty Eight in northern Alberta with twenty First Nations.

At the signing of the treaties in the late eighteen hundreds, each family was given one quarter section of land. With the exception of the Hobbema four tribes, the land assigned to the natives was extremely poor soil or muskeg. Each family received an ox and a plough, and each member five dollars per year in treaty money from the crown, which has not increased since, and is still handed out on treaty day.

The government agreed to take care of their well being, including health, education, and the upkeep of housing. Education was gradually provided in federal schools on reserves, the children were not allowed to speak their language or to practice their culture and traditional ceremonies. Later, in the mid nineteen hundreds, many children had to attend religious schools, away from their parents and extended families, where physical punishment was a daily occurrence. Sexual abuse in these schools happened often, which has been admitted today by various church groups and the federal government. Since these abuses are before the courts today, I cannot elaborate on these cases.

However, it is my belief that the treatment of natives in those days and up to about nineteen hundred sixty was consciously exercised to assimilate them into the white society, have them lose their identity, culture, and heritage, and establish a lower class of Canadian citizen.

In those days the native people were not allowed to leave the reserves, and over the years living conditions were similar to those in ghettos.

When I talk about the short sightedness of our forefathers, it is very clear that they did not forecast the population growth on reserves, which in most cases is now tenfold that of one hundred twenty years ago. In the beginning the population decreased due to influenza and chickenpox, which was brought in by the Europeans. The immune system of the natives could not ward off these new diseases, but after several decades the population started to grow again. Today the native population increases by about seven percent annually, compared to less than two percent in the Caucasian population.

Today the federal government is in a dilemma. The budget of the Indian affairs department runs into the billions, the taxpayers grumble, in particular since natives don't have to pay taxes if they are treaty Indian. Any First Nation that owns their own business does not have to pay business tax or G.S.T., and they usually locate all their administrative services on the reserve.

Most reservations have their own service stations now, so their members don't pay federal or provincial tax on gasoline or tobacco goods.

Over decades the federal government has used the band-aid approach for anything that was lacking on reserves. Money will not solve the many problems that exist, mainly housing, economic development, and social problems.

Curiously the strides that have been made over the past twenty years, in particular in the area of education, have had some negative effects, and added to the federal government's dilemma. Education has been most positive to the native population in so far that they have their own teachers, lawyers, social workers, and health service providers; it has given first nations the opportunity to deliver their own programs, and to decide their own destiny. The negative in all this is that it also created a new breed of politicians, some of whom have become more crooked, and devious than their white counterparts. While the federal government wants to abolish the outdated Indian act, and replace it with a new, revised version, while the feds want to accommodate first nations in regards to their quest for self government, most proposals are rejected by the chiefs and their councils.

They would like it both ways, they want the money, but they also want continuous protection under the Indian act. While native politicians pretend to listen and to follow their Elder's advice, they go their own way, by squandering millions of government dollars. Business meetings must be held in the most expensive hotels, conferences on various programs usually take place in Las Vegas, Nevada or high priced resort towns. Yet lectures are very seldom attended by the participants, they are out to have a good time. It is not uncommon to have twenty to fifty conference participants from just one reserve, who receive one hundred fifty to two hundred dollars U.S. as a daily expense allowance, besides the first class flights and hotel accommodations.

The next ten to twenty years should prove interesting. In my opinion there has to be a new arrangement between the federal government and the first nations. However, a new or revised Indian act is not the solution. To have five hundred plus first nations is ludicrous, it is ridiculous to have all these tiny countries within Canada, some with a population of less than two hundred, yet with their own administrative structure, and highly paid chiefs and counsellors. We could possibly have one large First Nation in the east, and one in the west, since some First Nations in the east are farther advanced than those in the west. To muddy the situation further, most reserves in B.C. have no treaties. Most chiefs reject the idea of having reserves become municipalities, such as Sechelt in B.C, although the government of Canada would like nothing better. Many reserves still follow a two year election cycle, which is not conducive to stability, and good business practices. On most reserves there exist two or three dominant families; they are usually the privileged ones, as chiefs and councils are elected from their ranks on most occasions.

Also, I believe that many of the wealthy reserves, those that were fortunate enough to have oil discovered on their land, should become more self sufficient, and finance their own programs. Invest properly, and create more businesses to support their own population. They should implement their own tax system. It is unfortunate, but I have seen reserves where the dominant families and the politicians, live in mansions, own two or more SUVs and luxury cars, the ladies wearing expensive fur coats, while the majority of the band members live in very poor conditions, and/or are on social assistance, so from that point of view, it's not all that different from the white society.

The biggest problem natives face is discord among themselves. There is no unity between the various tribes or First Nations, and is very similar to the situation among Arab countries. Of course, the federal government fosters disunity. Divided they fall, etc. What the feds don't seem to realize is, that this does not solve anything, and on the long run it is very unhealthy for all of Canada.

When I started my job at Enoch, I soon realized that this was tailor-made for me, as I could benefit from my expertise and personal strengths. I had expertise in all facets of life, e.g. farming, construction, business administration, personnel management, above all the use of common sense. My personal strengths are a positive attitude, determination, decision making, communication, and the knack to mediate and negotiate. Most of all I am a good listener, and have no problems to adjust to any situation. I am able to relate to people in power, and equally so to the less fortunate, as well as people with personal problems. My success working with native people was my ability to gain their trust, and that is what I always set out to do. I involved Elders in all my ideas, I involved myself in their celebrations, and spiritual ways, by attending sweats, participating in the sun dance, and sweet grass ceremonies, I was invited to attend important functions, where the sacred peace pipe was passed around, and became myself a believer in the native philosophy to love and share. In later years there was always a struggle among band members and the leadership regarding the traditional ways, and the born-again Christians. I always sided with the traditionalists. Over the decades our native people have come to mistrust the white man, and with reason, even today there exists a lot of discrimination when it comes to equal opportunities. Gaining the trust of the majority of band members and their leadership made my job so much easier.

The Enoch Chief and council decided to transfer all responsibilities and authorities regarding all departments to me, in their endeavour to establish a management system separate from the political arena. On most other reservations, each councillor accepted a portfolio for each program area. Under the rules at that time, the number of elected counsellors was based on population. For each one hundred band members we elected one counsellor. That changed in later years, as the population grew rapidly, and it would not have been economically feasible to support some fifteen to twenty councillors, so most reserves started to cap the number of elected officials.

I started to train some young, promising band members in the management field, and had them report to me as apprentices. Council meetings were held two days per week, and I attended all of them, that was my official reporting system to the Chief and council. Enoch in those days was a very wealthy community with an abundance of oil producing wells. Geologists warned us in those days that most of the wells would stop producing within a six year period, which gave us some time to plan ahead for the economic future of the reserve. We purchased a thirty quarter section Hutterite colony with about two thousand hogs, for four million dollars, started a nine hundred head cow/calf operation, and constructed very modern facilities. We also purchased a motel in Stony Plain, Alberta and added banquet rooms, a cocktail lounge, and beer parlors. At the Colony we converted one of the Hutterite houses into a substance abuse treatment centre for young people. Personally I thought we were doing pretty well and moving in the right direction, however, our Chief had grandiose ideas and told me I had to think much bigger, he wanted to get into the business of horse racing, and made trips to Japan to drum up investments from that country, which of course never materialized. In addition to this, he was addicted to gambling, and often disappeared for days to Las Vegas, while I had scheduled meetings with business people from Alberta and B.C. The first cracks in our relationship started to appear, and although I had the support of six of the seven Councillors, communication between the Chief and myself was at an all time low. At the same time we were constructing a very modern Administration Building at a cost of two million dollars, the Council Chamber was a show piece, the desks were made of solid oak and the chamber featured a mural which cost eighty thousand dollars to paint. Enoch also belonged to the Yellow Head Tribal Council (Y.T.C.), a group of five First Nations, which was founded in 1977. It was felt that power was in numbers, even more so if you were united in your goals and objectives. Over the years more tribes formed these types of Councils all over the Province.

Their meetings were held regularly once per month and member bands of the Y.T.C. consisted of the Alexander, Alexis, Enoch, O'Chiese and Sunchild Tribes. The meetings were always well attended by the Chiefs and Councillors with the exception of Enoch, whose Chief felt that the Tribal Council had really nothing to offer to them, as Enoch at that time was one of the wealthiest Reserves per capita, while the other four member bands were struggling to become more successful. I was the lone representative from Enoch during those meetings, and became the only "White Man" in the Province of Alberta, who had the privilege to cast a vote during those meetings. In later years the Y.T.C. became a very important and successful organization both, economically and politically. I was involved with them in an advisory capacity for years to come, as a representative of the Alexis First Nation, where I spent the next twelve years.

I left Enoch on good terms, and still run in to some of my management trainees, who have all become successful, some in the field of management and business, others in the political arena. Two or three years after I left, Enoch went through a very difficult time financially, they lost the Hutterite Colony, the hotel, the race horses and other investments. I am glad to see that they have started to make progress again, and did become a contributing member of the Y.T.C. Today they are operating a successful golf course, and are planning for a Casino—Hotel Resort complex which the City of Edmonton is opposed to.

During my last month at Enoch, the Y.T.C. organized a week long tour of the Navajo Nation for members of the five Nations, to see first hand how success can be achieved through education, good management and determination. Of course the Navajo had a two hundred year advantage on its Canadian relatives, however, it was an eye opener to all of us and their achievements were impressive. Enoch chartered their own plane, while the other four bands took the regular flight to Phoenix, Arizona. There we rented several vehicles in order to travel all parts of the Navajo Nation, which stretches from New Mexico through Arizona into Utah. Enoch rented two Cadillacs while the others made do with a sixteen passenger van, they called us the Mafia. The population of the Navajo Nation is about 1.5 million; they have their own capital at Window Rock, and have their own college, hospital, hotels, etc. The college besides the regular curriculum also teaches native medicine and healing. What was most impressive was that 90 percent of their young people graduated from Senior High School, and at that time, 1983, they had more than three hundred students enrolled at various Universities, the majority at the University of New Mexico in Albuquerque. The Navajo had constructed a sixty million dollar irrigation system and grew thousands of acres of corn and also hay for their cattle, and still had an abundance of produce to sell to other states, all this in the middle of the desert. Mining was another source of income, but their well educated and productive human resources were their biggest assets. Social assistance was available only to the elderly, single mothers with small infants, and those incapable to work for health reasons. If work was not readily available in areas where these individuals lived, they were relocated to areas such as the farming operation and/or the mines. This was not done at the request of the U.S. Government, these were the rules established by the Navajo authorities. The Grand Chief and his Council ran their Nation completely like an independent state; as a matter of fact their ambition was to become independent, with the Grand Chief having the status of a Governor.

The whole trip was very educational and it gave me many ideas what could be achieved with our Canadian Native people. However, reality is that today more than ever discord, dependency on the Government in Ottawa, too much interference by the Department of Indian Affairs, and Government unwillingness to make a serious attempt to support Native Self Government and Self Determination, is preventing our native people to achieve their aspirations. For decades the Federal Government has been using the "Band Aid" approach which has become more costly from year to year, and has not accomplished anything. The Billions wasted would have been better utilized by channelling it toward Native Self Government. The following suggestions may not be fully appreciated by some Native politicians, but in my humble opinion it is the only way to success.

The Treaties should be abolished and should be replaced by legal negotiated terms of co-existence between Canada and First Nations. The old treaties are no longer feasible to adhere to and have become a hindrance to progress.

Five Hundred and more independent First Nations in Canada are impossible to manage. The Native People in Canada must unite into two major self governing bodies, East and West. Each independent state would be comprised of approximately two hundred fifty tribes, and will be governed by a head of state elected every four years by the Tribal Chiefs from eastern or western Canada respectively. The two head of States will attend all First Ministers Conferences, and must have a mandate from their Tribal Chiefs to speak on their behalf.

Funding for Self Government must be provided based on the number of "have not" reserves within each state, and based on population. Self Government includes Administration, Education, Health, Economic Development, Child welfare and Social programming. First Nation Governments must implement their own tax system, and after the construction of adequate housing on reserves, houses should be purchased, leased or rented as in other societies.

Some may say this is going to be too expensive to the Government and therefore the tax payer, what is more costly, to continue paying Billions that keep on increasing year after year with no results, or to bite the bullet and pay heavily once. I personally doubt if many more additional dollars will be needed anyway, the present budget of the Department of Indian Affairs is humongous, this is one Department that has experienced a steady budget increase, never a budget cut. This new arrangement would eliminate several thousand highly paid bureaucrats not only in Ottawa but in every Provincial Capital, which would mean millions of dollars saved annually and could become part of the Self Government package; it would also force more than five hundred First Nations in Canada to become more accountable and to stop wasting money. I realize that my ideas will not sit well with either the Federal Government, due to the fact that several thousand high paid jobs will have to be eliminated, nor will it be popular with most native leaders as they would lose the Treaties, written and signed when Canada was a Colony. The treaties have become an albatross and are most detrimental to true

Self Government and Self Determination. I have also come to realize that over the years my views, proposals and suggestions that I have made many moons ago, have eventually come to fruition. Proposals I made in the early eighties materialized in the nineties. I have always been able to see years ahead, which irritates some people, but can also be beneficial. I strongly believe that when you plant a seed, it will germinate and grow, sometimes very slow, it all depends how you nourish and protect it. The most important factor is not to give up, it matters not how fragile and small that little plant is today. What I am saying is this I hope I planted a new seed and live long enough to see it come to fruition.

The Native leadership has a responsibility toward their people, to put their own egos aside, to not stand in the way of progress and to guide their people into the Twenty First Century. This does not mean to abandon their culture and their spirituality, it is to the benefit of mankind for native people to preserve and maintain their rich and beautiful heritage.

The reason I feel so passionately about this issue, is that during my work with the Native People of Canada I have met leaders that were not deserving to be called that, in the mid nineties for example, I worked for three Chiefs, who proposed to keep their people on Welfare, they asked me to keep the welfare roll high, as the Government contributions were based on a quota system. This to me was the height of a leaders irresponsibility, but let me continue with that part of my story later, as of now we are still in 1983.

Toward the end of having travelled all across the Navajo Nation, we visited the City in the Sky, a village built on top of a mountain about five hundred years ago. It was a fortress, accessible only by one narrow and steep mountain road. The Hopi Indians had built it centuries ago to defend themselves against other Indian Tribes. Very few people still lived there, mainly to keep the souvenir shops going, the bakery and some other establishments were kept open to serve the tourists. It was truly amazing how solid the old buildings still were, even though exposed to sometimes severe weather conditions on top of that mountain, and the view from the mountain was spectacular. There was also an old church extremely well preserved, legend has it that Hopi warriors carried all the wooden beams needed for the framework of the church, hundreds of miles across the desert and up to the mountain top. I believe this to be true for there are no trees for hundreds of miles in the desert.

Shortly after our return from the Navajo the time had come to say "Goodbye" to my friends at Enoch. The Chief's outlook in regards to the future development of the reserve, and my views were so different, that in time it would have hurt any progress we had made. Six of the seven councillors asked me to stay on but my mind was made up. Through my involvement with the Y.T.C. I had been able to gain the trust and respect of the other member Tribes leaders and the door was open for me to start work with any of the Tribes. But first I wanted to take some time off and follow my old dream farming on my own, also I wanted to do some physical work again, my mind was sharp but not my body.

I sold the acreage at Glen Park and purchased a one quarter section of bush land near Mayerthorpe. Over the next six month I was able to build a cabin, a small hog barn and fenced the land all with the help of two of the foster sons who were still with me. I dug a water well by hand; there was no running water, gas or power on the place, all that had to wait. I also built some corrals and still had two milk cows and six horses from Glen Park. Next I purchased forty Wiener pigs from two lady friends who operated a large hog farm near Westlock; we are still close friends to this day, even though they eventually sold the farm and moved to B.C. As a matter of fact my circle of friends increased during those days, durable friends, not fair weather friends or acquaintances. Through David who farmed only twelve miles from me, I met a very nice young woman, who was a nurse by profession, but also farmed and raised cattle, horses and sheep in the Beaumont area. In those days our involvement was more through our interest in farming, however in later years our friendship became much closer. Another friendship that survived time is Dale who grew up on a farm near Mayerthorpe and later in life moved to Edmonton. We share a love for all plant life and landscaping, he specializes in raising orchids. I did stray a little of my subject, but wanted to show the reader that although I live the life of a solitary man, I developed and cherished friendships that lasted all through my life. Of course I still had two foster sons and raised a few more over the next ten years.

I kept twenty potentially productive females from the forty pigs that I purchased and had real good luck with them. It was time to return to my consulting and advisory work to keep me mentally sharp, and also to have an income.

I incorporated my own Consulting Company working with First Nations on a contract basis. My first contract was with the Alexis First Nation in the Community Health field, little did I know that the Chief and his people would keep me busy for a period of twelve years, working with and advising the Chief and Council in the areas of Economic Development, Social Development, Child Welfare, Education, Elder Support and most of all obtaining financial support from the Federal and Provincial Governments for our projects. Among the people that interviewed me initially was a native lady by the name of Gladys, she was a Band Councillor. Gladys was married to the Chief's brother and the most wonderful human being you could meet anywhere. She had encountered many hardships as a young girl, but came through it all with a positive outlook on life and became very successful personally and professionally. Gladys lost a young daughter during my tenure at Alexis, and I had to admire her poise and inner strengths at that difficult time.

The Alexis Nation had no natural resources, and yet in many ways we were more successful than some of the wealthy Tribes. I have switched to "We" as during those twelve years I became a part of the community and was respected like a Band Member, it became my second home. Alexis had a resource of people who were rich in tradition and practiced their spirituality, not just by mouth but in their day to day life. Their Chief Howard Mustus was one of the most sincere and honest politicians I had ever met. He became one of the longest serving Chiefs in Canada, by the time I left Alexis twelve years later, he had been Chief for sixteen years. His success was based on true caring, love for his people, common sense and political savvy. His support came from the different large families on the reserve, as he himself could not fall back on a large family clan. We became friends and our relationship was much closer than that of a Superior and Subordinate.

At Alexis I blossomed, at most times I was given free reign to do the tasks that would help the community and the people. I always could count on the support of the Chief and Council and the people. I also involved myself in community activities, traditional celebrations, feasts and ceremonies, in their moments of joy as well as in moments of their grief.

I quickly realized that in order to be successful in my field, you needed the support of politicians, in particular a politician with clout. Alexis was located on the shores of Lac Ste. Anne, near the village of Onoway. It was a beautiful scenic setting; there were also two islands in the lake just waiting to be developed for tourism. In the meantime I also purchased a lake front property near the Alexis Reserve, which I used on week ends and to entertain certain politicians, business people and others that could further the cause of the Alexis Nation. Our M.L.A. for that area was Barrhead's Ken Kowalski, at that time the Deputy Premier, and Minister of Lotteries. I approached Ken on many occasions for various funding requests and found him to be very supportive if he could see that my proposals had merit and would have a positive effect on the First Nation's economy. He visited Alexis on several occasions, and at election time I could always assure him of several hundred votes from our population. I always campaigned openly on his behalf, and even though Treaty Indians frowned upon voting in Provincial elections, I was able to convince them that for the benefit of the Reserve, it was important that they voted. I became a card carrying member of the Provincial

P.C. party, even though I voted Liberal in Federal elections. I also joined Ken's Executive Board of Directors in Barrhead, and sold the homestead in Mayerthorpe in order to move into Ken's Constituency. Therefore I purchased a three quarter section well established farm near Barrhead with a beautiful home, and started a cattle and hog operation. Now I worked fulltime at Alexis, did consulting work for other Bands and the Y.T.C., looked after an eighty head cow/calf operation, some twenty sows that produced five hundred piglets per year, and worked on behalf of the P.C. party. Those were the most productive years of my life, and I enjoyed it. During the haying and calving season I always hired some help, quite often young people from the Reserve.

The people at Alexis were Stoney and were related to the Sioux, I found their way of life and their beliefs much more to my way of thinking, and would have done anything to help them in their aspirations. During those years of progress we were able to construct a Community Hall, Seniors Lodge, developed one of the islands, build many new homes, and started a large farm operation and above all constructed a beautiful new school, Kindergarten to Grade 12. We were able to include an Industrial Arts program and negotiated a contract for all native students who attended Provincial schools off Reserve. It took many trips to Ottawa to convince the Indian Affairs Minister of the need for this school, but we finally did it.

In the meantime the five member Bands of the Y.T.C. decided to take over all child welfare programs for our native children under the Y.T.C. umbrella. Too many native children became lost in the "White" system, grew up in non native foster homes, losing their culture, language and their identity. I have seen native children return to their Reserves at age eighteen; completely lost they were unable to cope with life on Reserve and did not fit in with either society and finally turned to activities that hurt their future destiny. Suicide was not uncommon; sometimes it seemed to be their only way out. We set up a Steering Committee comprised of two members each from the five First Nations, me being the Chair. For a period of two years we met once per week, and developed the framework for the takeover, the wording of the agreements with the two Governments and the organizational structure. All this became a very delicate process; we had to consider financial, political and cultural issues and incorporated those in the agreements. First Nations did not recognize Provincial jurisdiction, as their Treaties were signed with the Crown before the Province was in existence, however, Ottawa had transferred all Child Welfare responsibility to the Provinces in 1966 without consideration for native children. A lot of headaches could have been prevented, if the Feds would have shown some foresight and if the native leadership would have been as assertive in those days as they are today. After two years of hard work my Steering Committee and I completed our assignment, had it approved by our legal advisors and presented it to the respective Chiefs and Councillors, they voted unanimously to approve both documents to be signed by the respective Federal and Provincial Ministers.

The day of the signing was a big day in all our lives but most important for the native children. There was a Peace Pipe Ceremony, a Pow Wow, Round dance and feast. All the Chiefs wore their traditional Head Dress; there were Fancy Dancers, Grass Dancers and Jingle Dancers, all in their beautiful traditional costumes. Each Tribe was handed a beautiful crafted framed poster with the printed Mission Statement in Cree, Stoney, Saultaux and English. One of the statements on the document is my very own, that I had insisted on to be included, it read that each Native Child must be given the opportunity to develop to the utmost of its potential. The Prime Minister at the time was Joe Clark, who also happened to be the M.P. for Yellow Head, came for a special celebration and Pow Wow to Alexis, and of course told us that we should all be proud of our accomplishments.

When Don Getty announced that he would get out of politics, the race for the P.C. party leadership was on. In a special meeting of the Directors in Barrhead, Ken Kowalski gave an assessment of all the candidates and it was decided to support Ralph Klein in his bid to become the new leader. Of the two front runners, Nancy Betkowski (McBeth), and Ralph Klein, he said, "Anyone but her" and of Ralph, "he wants it so bad, he can taste it". I suggested that Ken should throw his hat in the ring, why should it be always someone from Calgary or Edmonton, let's give somebody from Rural Alberta a chance. Ken was an experienced politician, he was honest and sincere and would have had a lot of support in rural Alberta; however, he declined. Personally I did not like the idea of supporting Ralph Klein, in my opinion he is an opportunist, proven by the fact that he switched from the Liberal to the P.C. party when he realized that the Liberals would not go anywhere in Alberta. I believed he was a wolf in sheep's clothing and could not be trusted, unfortunately later events proved me right again. However, I supported Ken and toed the party line, for Alexis it was the right decision.

After the first run-off in Calgary, Nancy was ahead by one vote. Now Ken went into action, he mobilized the support of all rural M.P.s on Ralph's behalf, and asked me to bring the native vote out. I was able to organize four busloads of Alexis band members, gave the electoral officer in Onoway a blank company cheque, to pay for the P.C. membership of the several hundred voters from Alexis, and the rest they say is history. Ralph Klein did become Premier. Out of gratitude, he supported the Alexis First Nation very generously in their land claim, which at that time was a high priority for the chief. At the Alexis Pow Wow in July, King Ralph made an appearance by helicopter, I believe to avoid any media attention, and presented a one million dollar cheque to the chief and council.

At a later meeting I had with Ken in his office, he expressed the desire to become an honorary chief, and I promised my support, although at that time I was already contemplating leaving Alexis, and had hoped that I might be considered for the honour of honorary chief, but I never mentioned this to anybody. I approached the chief and council as well as the Elders with the proposal to bestow the honour of honorary chief to Ken Kowalski, and it was agreed to make it come true. This honour is something very special and takes a lot of planning. I believe Ken became the only non-native in Alexis's history who was granted his wish.

The Elders made all the ceremonial clothing fitting for a Chief, complete with headdress, and he was honoured at a special pipe ceremony followed by a Pow Wow, Round Dance, and feast.

His ceremonial outfit now is in Ken's office at the legislature.

The reason for my wanting to leave Alexis, after twelve years of successful service, was mainly due to the fact that I was tired, and I felt that there was not much more I could accomplish. I was sixty years old, and opposition to Howard's leadership had grown after the last election. A very strong religious group did not agree with his traditionalism, and gave him quite a run for his re-election for another term. As I was seen as his biggest supporter, I had to take the brunt of many verbal attacks. The opposition at one time staged a week long sit-in at the administration office.

When I announced to the chief and council my decision to leave, they tried to persuade me to stay. The chief sent Elders to my office to see if they could change my mind. It was very difficult for me to stick to my decision. This was home to me, I had seen school children grow up to be adults, I had seen what dedication, determination, and a strong belief could accomplish in a community that did not possess many riches. There were times when I had been asked by groups of band members to run for chief, which under the Indian Act was possible. However, I declined. Howard was my friend, and the best chief for Alexis. Also, my personal feeling is that no outsider should ever be chief in a native community. No matter how familiar you become with native tradition, ceremonies, and spirituality, you can believe in it, and practice it, but you will never be able to truly understand their ways.

My last day was one of the most emotional days in my life. Unbeknown to me, the band had secretly arranged for a feast and round dance. Speeches were made by the leaders, Elders, and ordinary band members. One of the Elders went so far as calling me a holy man, which of course embarrassed me greatly. My proudest moment came when one of the Elders presented me with an eagle feather, and the round dance started. I had tears in my eyes, when proudly carrying the feather, the chief and I followed by the council members, led the procession.

I have visited Alexis a few times when I lived in southern Alberta. Unfortunately these occasions were not always joyful, as the occasion for these visits was sometimes the funeral of a friend.

After I left, Howard did not run for re-election after his term was over. He became the executive director of the Yellowhead Tribal Council. My friend Gladys is the director of healthcare, and many of the young people have been successful in their life, hopefully, I have had some positive impact on their lives.

In the mid eighties Mom had lost her common-law husband, and returned to central Alberta where she bought a little house in Rockford Bridge, near Mayerthorpe, which gave me a chance to visit her often. I spent a lot of time with her, took her shopping, etc. She was very lonely, since most of her children lived now in B.C. and visited once a year. Cecilia, the youngest, lived in north eastern Alberta, and David, who was close by visited, but was very busy with his farm. Mom's health was failing, and she went into the Mayerthorpe lodge. When I moved to my farm in Barrhead, I could see her only once every week. In 1993 she passed away, alone. That upset me more than anything. She had always expressed the desire to move in with me; however, David talked her out of it, saying that I was too busy to look after her, etc. I blamed myself for not insisting that she live with me. I would always have found the time to look after her. After all, she had been my Mom for over thirty years when she died, and I loved her very much. At her funeral I was inconsolable. Another loved one left me.

I sunk a lot of money into the farm; practically everything I earned went to the purchase of haying equipment and other machinery. I also purchased some purebred Simmenthal cows. The help I hired during haying and calving I could not depend on, a lot of machinery was broken through carelessness. However, today I wish that I would have held on to the place, I loved it, I loved my animals and the buildings were very nice. A two thousand square foot, four bedroom house, a large Quonset and barn, and cattle shelters, everything was in prime condition. The landscaping was very nice, the house set on a hill overlooking all the land around it. In the summer I had regular Bar B Q's for neighbours, friend, and some politicians. Ena and Francis came every year, and stayed a few days. For the parties I always invited my foster sons. One was married now, and had children of his own. So I was a grandpa now. One summer Ena's daughter Gail and her son Ryan also visited. Ryan was about four at that time and had never been on a farm, but walked right among the cattle and had me worried that the bull might attack him; however, my cattle were so tame that they did not pay much attention to him. It was a different story when I gave him a ride on my tractor, he screamed bloody murder, and I was unable to pacify him.

Six month after leaving Alexis, I decided to take on another contract with three Tribes at Morley in Southern Alberta. Against my better judgement I sold the farm with all the equipment and livestock. Needless to say two years after I sold out, land and cattle prices soared. Why do people make irrational decisions? I have always been an excellent Manager and decision maker for companies and First Nations I worked for, but usually took a loss when handling my own affairs. I blame it on my restless life, on not having roots, in the past twenty years I had owned and sold eight different properties, the six years on the farm, was the longest I had stayed in one place. Now I was sixty one and still not settled down.

My new job was on the Morley Reservation, on the Trans Canada highway between Calgary and Banff, a most beautiful setting. The Morley Reserve consisted of three Tribes, totalling some three thousand people, living in three different locations, Morley, Eden Valley and Big Horn. I was the Director of Social Development and Child Welfare, in total seven programs, with a budget of about eleven million dollars annually, and reported to three Chiefs. These Chiefs were the political heads of the Goodstoney, Chiniki and Bearspaw Tribes. It was extremely difficult and took all my communication skills to keep all three Chiefs happy, each one of them protecting their own interests. One Chief was an alcoholic and came to meetings intoxicated with a girlfriend at his side, one was too old and in poor health to be able to govern, but stubbornly held on to his position. The third Chief was the dominant one; he was power hungry and very devious, originally elected under the slogan, "Empowerment through Education". He never fulfilled his promises. Not well educated himself, his people had an average education level of grade seven.

I was under an annual contract, and did quite well for one year. I was the main Chief's favourite, who made him look good, and take his people to the 'Promised Land'. My accomplishments at Alexis had preceded me, as the people from Alexis and Morley were related and the only Stoneys in Alberta. The people at Morley were very poor and it was a much worse situation at Eden Valley and Big Horn, about ninety percent of the population were on Social Assistance. Despite the rhetoric and promises by the Chiefs, they really had no interest to change the situation, the more people on Welfare, the more money was forthcoming from the Department of Indian Affairs. The three tribes were a part of Treaty Seven, the other tribes being Siksika, Sarcee and Peigan; they tended to look down at their poor cousins from Morley. Most of them were better educated, had a superior business structure in place, and were well managed; Siksika is one of the most progressive First Nations in Canada.

My goal was to change the situation at Morley, the people there had a lot going for them, and they were eager and willing to better themselves but were held back by selfish politicians. All three Reserves were located in some of the most beautiful scenic parts of Canada; Morley had the most potential for economic development, particularly in the area of tourism and the hospitality field. Canmore was one of the fastest growing communities in the Rocky Mountains since the Calgary Olympics in 1988, and had the most objections to any development at Morley, "not in our backyard", they sad. The height of stupidity was however, when the Chiefs decided to hire the Mayor of Canmore as a part-time Director at Morley, in my opinion this was a conflict of interest situation, and he never should have sought or accepted such a position. Another problem was that the three tribes isolated themselves; they did not participate in Treaty Seven activities or any other meetings of various program areas with other tribal councils where a lot of planning and sharing of information took place. I started to attend Treaty Seven meetings and was well received, even though I was the only "white man" at those sessions. I also participated in all monthly meetings of the Native Child Welfare Agencies in Alberta, at that time there were twenty two incorporated agencies in Alberta, and our meetings usually resulted in some positive action regarding all native children in Alberta.

After my first year at Morley I had a surplus of one million dollars in my budget, under the negotiated five year Socio/Economic Development plan, I did not have to return any of that surplus to Indian Affairs. I contacted the Mount Royal Community College in Calgary and negotiated a contract with them to come to Morley and provide an upgrading program to twenty five selected adult students, followed by a two year Social Service Diploma program to the same students. I also provided financial support from that surplus to Band members who desired to attend Colleges and/or Universities away from home. My contract had been renewed for an additional year by the three Chiefs before they knew that I had a surplus, and how I intended to use it. One of the big success stories was a young lady, Terry Fox, the daughter of Tina Fox, one of the most honest and sincere politicians at Morley with a lot of foresight and concern for the future of her people. Terry had been the Manager of the Woman's Shelter and I groomed her to be my successor, she left home to attend the University of Victoria in B.C. The main Chief, who wanted to empower his people through education, was very upset with me, and started to undermine my position. He questioned my decisions to take undeserving band members off the welfare roll, most of them were his supporters, and thereby saving all that money. He also felt that surplus should have been channelled in his direction for his own political endeavours. We had Band members that illegally sold big trees from the Tribe's beautiful forest to B.C. lumber companies, some of them making more than one hundred thousand dollars per month, yet had the nerve to call my Social Workers on their Cell phones from their brand new SUV's to inquire if their welfare cheque was ready.

My contract was renewed twice, after the third year however, my favourite Chief refused to sign it. I had become too popular, and with the support of Tina Fox and some other conscientious politicians, I was able to take people of the welfare roll, provide them with jobs, and help them further their education. Some of the Chief's supporters saw the light and turned against him, he started to get worried about the next election. I was still at Morley on that great day when twenty three of our students graduated from Mount Royal College, and I felt very fortunate to see those proud and happy faces. When I left, Tina Fox and I embraced, crying on each others shoulder, worried that the progress we had achieved would be lost again, but once again the seed had been planted. The next election none of the three Chiefs was re-elected, two years later a big investigation was initiated by a judge from Calgary, regarding mismanagement of millions of dollars, why the majority of the population lived in poverty, while over the years they had received much more than was needed, and with proper management they could have been at par with the other Treaty 7 Nations. As a result Morley was placed under Trustee ship and managed by a consulting firm for a period of two years. I was called by the major news media from Calgary and Edmonton to provide them with the inside scoop, but refused. I was just very sad, so many wonderful people at Morley with a lot of potential and dreams for the future, made one mistake, they elected the wrong Chiefs.

`I kept on attending the Child Welfare Agency meetings, even though I was not affiliated with any particular Tribal Council or First Nation, although I did the odd consulting work for various Tribes. I wanted to officially retire, but my mind was changed for me. At one of the meetings I met a native lady who was in charge of Child Welfare at the Louis Bull First Nation at Hobbema, she told me that two of the Hobbema Nations, namely Louis Bull and Montana, wanted to take control of all Child Welfare services from the Province, however, after three years of research, planning and preliminary work, they had not been able to get anywhere with the negotiators from the Province, although they employed the services of two legal advisors. They were running out of time and funding to continue and needed somebody right now. She asked me if I would be willing to write and negotiate a Services Agreement with the Province as well as a financial five year agreement with Ottawa on their behalf. When I indicated my willingness, she asked me to fax a brief resume to their Board of Directors, and they in all likelihood would call me in return to have a talk with me.

These child welfare agencies were usually headed by a board of directors, appointed by the chiefs, as the chiefs refused to negotiate with the provinces.

Within two days I had a call to come to the Bearspaw truck stop on highway #2 near Wetaskiwin, which was owned by the Louis Bull tribe. There I met with the board for lunch. This was September 1, 1996 and we agreed that I would start after the Labour Day long weekend. They had received an additional twenty five thousand dollars from Indian Affairs to come to an agreement with the Province by years end. That gave me less than four months, with time off for the Christmas holidays.

In our first negotiation meeting, I realized that the main obstacle to reach an agreement was the administrator of social services for Wetaskiwin. She was a very abrupt, domineering person, and all four Hobbema reserves were under her jurisdiction, regarding child welfare. I knew her well, for it was me that had recruited her twenty three years before, when I was still with the Province. She definitely was not included in my ninety five percent success rate in hiring people. I contacted the minister of Alberta Family Services, at that time Stockwell Day, and asked that she be removed from the negotiation team; he accommodated me and replaced her with a much more positive person. From then on the negotiations went smoothly. We were done on December 22, and were the first agency that had a Provincial agreement that recognized native traditions and spirituality equal to the child welfare act.

Under the agreement there was a six month implementation period, which required that a director be hired, who would be responsible to write all policies, procedures, job descriptions. Recruit and train staff, negotiate a time frame with the provincial offices to transfer the files of all children that were Louis Bull and Montana band members. It was also my objective to train a suitable member from either one of these two reserves to eventually take over from me.

The board asked me to stay on as director for at least one year, and I agreed, which meant to sell my property in southern Alberta and look for something else in the Wetaskiwin area. During the four months I worked on the agreement and the negotiations, I had lived out of my suitcase, and stayed at a motel in Millet, I liked that town. When I was offered the director's position, I rented a very nice two bedroom apartment in Wetaskiwin. All the while I worked at Hobbema I kept on looking for a suitable property to retire on, again.

Things went very smoothly for more than one year; so I recruited a young lady from the Montana tribe to become my understudy. She had gone to the Leth-bridge University, and had the dedication, purposefulness, and personality to become a very successful director. In May we had a big feast, ceremony, and round dance, to celebrate the takeover. The Board of Directors presented me with a framed print of one of the native artists masterpieces. The original adorns the new Montana school. In December 1997 my contract was renewed for another year, during that year I was going to let Eunice run the agency by herself, and only fill in during her absence. My appointment, and delegation of ministe-rial authority from Mr. Day, did not expire till June 1998.

Then in February everything went array. Politics took precedent over the well being of children.

Among all the files transferred from the provincial offices to us, I noticed two files that were extremely bulky, they were transferred from the Rocky Mountain House district office, and involved two girls from the Louis Bull tribe, who were both in a native foster home in Red Deer. The girls now eight and nine years old, had allegedly been savagely raped by their grandfather, when they were three and four. According to the older siblings, the drunken mother and father, were in the next room passed out, when all this happened. According to paediatricians and other physicians reports, one of the girls would never be able to have children; the other had torn muscles in her anus, both girls contacted gonorrea.

I was sick to my stomach; I went to Rocky Mountain House to talk to the social workers there. They told me that they had tried to bring the matter to court, but did not get very far, one of the girls could barely talk, the other one had been burned with a lighter, by her mother to keep quiet. The grandfather was also related to some of the influential councillors on the reserve, who blocked every attempt to get enough evidence against him. I visited the girls in Red Deer; the foster mother was a very wonderful, caring native woman. She told me the girls were acting out sexually; one still had a speech problem. She also told me that they were afraid of older men, so I didn't expect that they would talk to me. When the girls arrived home from school, I found them to be quite open to me. We looked at photo albums and they showed me their Halloween costumes that their foster mother had made for them. Then one of them asked if I knew her mother, I said yes, and then she said my mother is bad, she always took me into the dark room and burnt me. I had to leave, and cried all the way back from Red Deer. By the way, the files also indicated that the girl did have burn marks on her buttocks and inner thighs when she was apprehended.

I took this whole matter to the next board of director's meeting, and told them that it was my responsibility to re-open the case, and bring the perpetrator to court. Originally eight of nine board members agreed. Some had known something, but did not know the details. The one disagreement was a councillor and also a relative of the accused. I doggedly would not let go, and a court date was set for late April in Red Deer. At the Louis Bull office all hell broke loose. The family started a vendetta against me, I ended up in shouting matches with a native lawyer who represented the children's parents, and wanted them returned to them. Our lawyer would only approve supervised visits from the parents. It was actually the father who now lived with another woman. The chief at Louis Bull, who had always supported me, and who was an ex-child welfare worker himself, lost the election. The new chief, a woman who didn't have a clue in politics, and who as an office worker previously, had always been one of the laziest and undependable employees, supported the family of the perpetrator, and even wrote to the judge trying to influence him, completely ignoring the fact that the chief and council had no jurisdiction in the area of child welfare. So she replaced the Louis Bull members of the board with new ones that were willing to listen to her. That was against the constitution as well. According to Boards by-laws, members had to resign in writing, then the director would send a request to the chief to replace these members. Regulations, constitutional issues, were thrown out the window when it came to family politics, and elections. To hell with children whose lives have been destroyed by a monstrous relative. Children cannot vote. It is in times like this when I lose faith in mankind.

The court hearing took place the first week in May. The girls and other siblings testified behind a screen, so they wouldn't have to see their grandfather. The judge decided that there was enough evidence to bring the case to trial. A small victory, but nothing could ever give these girls a normal life to live.

The following Monday I was let go, it was all done hush-hush, after the office closed, so that my staff wasn't aware of it. They all came to visit me in Wetaskiwin over the next few weeks, but I just wanted to forget, and above all rest. This was the end of my career.

7

Living One Day at A Time

On the Canada Day long weekend I attended the family reunion at Jack and Doris's in Cranbrook, B.C. It was three wonderful days and the weather was great. There was a horseshoe tournament that Jack's second eldest son Joe organized, and a golf tournament that my Godson John was in charge of, games from softball and volleyball for the kids that Ena looked after, a lot of food, and sing-a-longs in the evening lasting until four a.m. Rose had come from Australia; I hadn't seen her since 1971, almost thirty years. Doris had told Ena that Joe suffered from a lot of stomach pain, was losing weight, but always refused to see a doctor. Well, one month after the reunion it was discovered that Joe had cancer of the esophagus which had spread, and it was too late to operate. Joe suffered for another thirteen months, and passed away July 30th the next year. This was very hard on Jack and Doris; they were such a close-knit family. My Godson John took it harder than anybody, he and Joe were very close.

As I realized a few months after the reunion, Joe may have saved my life, because I did not wait to see a doctor when I had difficulty swallowing and started to lose weight. At Joe's funeral my cancer was already in remission, and I thought *'why him and not me'*. In September I was diagnosed with non-Hodgkin's Lymphoma, the same cancer that Mario Lemieux and Sako Koivu had overcome, and that Jackie Kennedy-Onassis died from. I had suffered a sore throat for about a month when I finally consulted my physician, who told me that my tonsils were badly swollen, and made an appointment with a specialist. He in turn told me that my tonsils had to be removed immediately. I thought it kind of funny to have your tonsils removed at my age that is normally done to children. Anyway, the next day they were removed electronically. It was very painful, and I didn't even get any ice cream.

Within a week the specialist called and told me that he had made an appointment with the Cross Cancer Institute, and I was to report there, they had discovered cancerous growths on my tonsils. I was familiar with the Institute, for the past six months I had worked as a volunteer with the seniors lodge in Warburg. Part of my duties was to drive seniors to doctors appointments and many of them had to be taken to the Cross Cancer Institute for appointments and treatment. I remember thinking "I hope I will never end up here", seeing the drawn, pale, and haggard faces of so many people with cancer, made me feel so small, sad, and inadequate. In particular, children with cancer, made me feel so helpless, and when I saw their small bodies, hairless heads, and their eyes expressing knowledge far beyond their age, I thought to myself *'why them, why not somebody like me who has lived his life, who is alone and wouldn't leave an empty seat at a family dinner'.*

So I went to my appointment, not all that anxious, ready to accept any diagnosis the specialist came up with. Of course, I went through all kinds of blood tests, an MRI, and X-rays; they even drilled a hole in my hipbone to extract some bone marrow. Then I had to see the Oncologist, who told me that they discovered Non-Hodgkin's in my lymph nodes on both sides of my neck. The prognosis was not very good; Non-Hodgkin's lymphoma is one of the second fastest spreading cancers. There are some two hundred lymph nodes in the human body, and if the disease spreads into your bone marrow, it's 'lights out'. He told me that if it has spread, I would have a fifty percent chance to live five more years. But we would have to wait for all the test results. I took all this very calmly, and familiarized myself with the idea of not living very much longer, that was OK!

One week later I was called back to the clinic to see the Oncologist. The first thing he said was, "You are a very lucky man." The cancer had not spread anywhere, and I would be cured through chemo-therapy, followed by thirty days of intense radiation treatment. When he gave me the good news, I broke down and just sobbed uncontrollably. It seems I can take bad news calm and collected, and become emotional when I hear good news. Weird or what? It seems that despite all the bravado of being ready to die, we seem to want to live more than we realize. This whole cancer issue put the idea of purchasing a retirement property on the backburner. My friend Mikki still worked as a nurse, she also farmed with a very close friend Annie, and they owned a lakefront cottage at Buck lake, which they spent some time at on weekends, and vacation, but seldom were off work on the same weekend. Annie had a very good job in Edmonton, but also worked very hard with their cow/calf operation on the farm near Millet.

They offered me to stay at their cabin at the lake, during my treatment period, and for my recovery after. The cabin was fully furnished and winterized, and I jumped at the idea. I gave all my furniture and other belongings to the church in Warburg, and moved out to Buck Lake in October.

I started my chemo treatment the following week, which was taken in five sessions in three week intervals I did not experience any serious side effects from the treatment. However, after about three weeks I lost all my hair from my head, arms, legs, armpits and pubic hair, my body was as smooth as a baby's.

Christmas, Mikki and Annie came out to the lake, and we had a nice dinner. On Boxing Day we went out to visit other friends and had another dinner. Although my appetite was not the greatest in those days, the food was good. New Years Eve the neighbours at the lake and us went ski-doing. Mikki and Annie had three ski-dos, so there was a spare one for me. We went across the lake, through bush trails, up and down hills, and stopped once in awhile to rest, and to have a sip from the flask, to keep our insides warm. We were gone for about eight hours, and I was exhausted. Sixty six years old, and a cancer patient, I also had lost about fifty pounds by that time.

Three days later I had to go to Edmonton for my last chemo session. Before each session they took a blood sample to check the patients white and red blood cell count, to see if the immune system could withstand the chemo treatment. As it turned out, they had to turn me back, and I had to wait another week, as my immune system was extremely low due to the strenuous day of ski-doing, but it was fun. I had felt like a kid again.

In February the radiation treatments started, five days per week for one full month. So I had to move into Edmonton for one month, and only drove to Buck Lake on weekends. I was fitted with a plastic mould from head to chest, and had to attend three fitting sessions until it was perfect. The radiation was given to both sides of my neck. I lost my sense of taste, all food tasted sour, even chocolates. My taste buds returned to almost normal after about six months; however, my saliva glands were no longer functional, even today after two years I suffer from dry mouth.

The staff at the Cross Cancer Institute deserves many kudos, and my two Oncologists, Dr. Belch and Dr. Pearcey, I consider the best. Since the completion of my treatments, I do go to the clinic every six months for follow-up tests, and am checked out by Dr. Pearcey. So far everything seems to be fine.

In March I started to look for my own place again, I would have loved to stay in the Buck lake area. It is beautiful country, hills and valleys, huge spruce trees everywhere, but also quite expensive. Five years earlier I could have afforded it, but not now.

I found a small two bedroom house with garage and a nice fenced lot in the village of Millet, a very scenic town, which is within commuting distance to Edmonton. As I got healthier, my old drive returned, and I wanted to do things.

To live in a small house, with a small garden, no animals to keep, was not for me. Also, having neighbours on each side of me became an annoyance. They were very nice people, as a matter of fact; the young couple on one side had their parents live on the other side of me. The father was a few years older than me, and it came to the point where I was reluctant to go into my garden. He was right there at the fence, and talked on and on. He had lived in Millet all his life, knew everybody, and told me the same stories over and over. I stayed exactly one year in Millet, and must have heard each story three hundred times. Don't get me wrong, I love people and have proven that over and over, I also like to talk to people, socialize and enjoy get-togethers, parties and picnics, but I need my space.

As I could ill afford to purchase a country property in that particular area, I started to travel around and looked at acreages East and North East of Edmonton, where the prices are more reasonable. The second property I looked at was exactly what I had in mind, a large spacious home, a nice fenced yard, beautiful trees and privacy. It consisted of four mostly treed acres which would provide a lot of wood for the fire place, and lots of opportunity for landscaping and gardening. I immediately fell in love with the property and purchased it. Both my neighbours on either side of me are two miles away; they are wonderful people and welcomed me to the neighbourhood. Although the nearest town of importance is Vegreville, with a population of mainly Ukrainian descent, most of the farmers in my area are of German background. My neighbour Terry's mother came originally from Bessarabia and speaks German. She had some of the same wartime experiences that I endured and also wrote about that part in her life.

Terry and Leanne are hardworking, decent people; they have three sons, who have been raised to respect others, and are very different from most teens that you meet in the Cities and Towns. Leanne always seems to be worried about me living alone, I am trying to convince her that this is the life I have chosen, and the life I want. The neighbours on the other side of me, Barry and Anita are always willing to lend a helping hand, they are hard working people, and both hold two jobs in town, besides farming. Barry is very outgoing, loves classical music, and enjoys talking politics, fortunately we are on the same wave lengths, and therefore we don't get into arguments.

This is the end of my life's story, I wanted to leave a record to show that I really existed and lived a life that was filled with tears and laughter, sorrows and joy, hurt and love, and that is the way it should be. However, my childhood and adolescent years should never be experienced by any child. When I leave this earth, I want a copy of this story placed in a weather and corrosion proof capsule, and want it buried in one of my beloved flower beds. If I ever win the lottery, I will make a trip to Europe and visit Oma and Opa's estate it is now possible to travel in to that part of Russia. If I had a choice, that is where I would want to die and be buried in the soil that belonged to my family for Centuries.

My Legacy is that I have been able to help many young people to have a brighter future, and have been able to give many Native Canadians the opportunity to develop themselves in accordance with their potential. I have been able to show them by my examples to set high standards and goals, and above all to be kind and giving, that is the best recipe for a successful life.

If by writing my story I have been able to convince some people that it is more desirable to be a leader rather than a follower and to stand up for the less fortunate, I will have accomplished something. If I have been able to make a few people realize that war is never the answer to make the world a better place to live in, I will have accomplished a lot. I may have also planted a seed in those that can see beyond today and believe in a better tomorrow, and just possibly, our universe may survive.

Yes, I believe in Utopia, all we have to do is dream and use all our thoughts, senses and strengths, to make these dreams come true.

Author's Biography

The author was born during the year Adolph Hitler came to power in Germany. He is the last descendent of a family whose roots go back to the Christian Crusaders, who invaded the Slavic countries of Eastern Europe in the thirteenth century, and decided to stay.

Due to the Second World War of 1939–1945, which devastated most of Europe, he lost his family, his home, and his planned future.

The author was reluctant to tell his story for more than fifty years, as it forced him to bare his soul and his innermost feelings. But as the last survivor of his family, and now seventy years of age, he felt that the time had come to tell all.

Down and out four times during his life, he always was able to survive, and with honesty and his love for all human beings he has remained a staunch believer in peace, and in love, and sharing with his fellow man.

He now is retired on an acreage in Eastern Alberta, and enjoys a quiet life of landscaping, gardening, and in the company of his pet animals.

0-595-29518-5